Killer in the New Forest

Also by Carol Cole

THE DI CALLUM MACLEAN MYSTERIES
Book 1: Murder in the New Forest
Book 2: Straw in the Wind
Book 3: Killer in the New Forest

Killer *in the* New Forest

The DI Callum MacLean Mysteries Book 3

Carol Cole

THE BOOK FOLKS

The Books Folks
A Joffe Books Company
www.thebookfolks.com

First published in Great Britain in 2025

This book is a work of fiction. Names, characters, businesses, organizations, places and events are either the product of the author's imagination or are used fictitiously. Any resemblance to actual persons, living or dead, events or locales is entirely coincidental. The spelling used is British English except where fidelity to the author's rendering of accent or dialect supersedes this.

ISBN: 978-1-80462-350-3

Prologue

He walks tentatively, uncertain of the ground beneath his feet. The January darkness has softened the contours of the heath. It has levelled the uneven surface and filled the hollows with black shadow. It confuses him. He followed this same path earlier in the day when the woody stems of heather had dragged at his jeans. Now they are iced stiff with frost and stick upwards, silver daggers stabbing at his legs.

The screaming bark of a fox cleaves the air and is swiftly followed by the alarmed call of a pheasant. He shivers. He does not understand this world with unseen predators out there in the gloom. The gorse bushes are inky silhouettes against the night sky like groups of silent watchers. He has the unsettling feeling that they are following his progress.

He stumbles over a broken branch that snaps beneath his foot, and he falls forward onto his knees. Close to the path, a small creature scurries through the dead bracken and in the distance the whinny of a wild pony is carried to him on the wind. He stays still, listening, but neither alarm him as much as the call of the hunting fox.

Regaining his feet, he fastens his jacket and glances up at the heavy sky. Earlier that day it had been clear but with nightfall, the clouds have gathered. Not the soft marshmallow depictions of children's drawings but a threatening ebony-based mass that scuds along, hugging the horizon and partially obliterating the distant trees. The sharp breeze that herds the clouds is cold enough to pierce flesh.

Ahead he sees house lights, knows he is nearly there and unconsciously touches his pocket. Suddenly, like some long-buried secret, the clouds drift apart and a deathly-pale moon bursts into view, lighting his way.

The next thing he knows for sure is that he is on all fours, gravel biting into the palms of his hands and stabbing through his jeans into the flesh of his knees. He hurts and is in too much pain to attempt to stand up. His head droops and his nostrils are filled with the smells of damp earth and horse droppings. He takes a shaky breath, and pain explodes inside his chest like a fireball. That's when he realises the unfamiliar taste in his mouth is blood.

Behind him, he hears footsteps and raises his head as they approach but only manages a whispered plea for help that goes unheeded. The footfalls are rhythmic and relentless, scrunching over the small stones like an incoming tide creeping up a pebble beach. The moon appears through a break in the clouds and throws a spotlight on him. It is so bright that the sharp shadow is as clear as a black-and-white movie. He sees the figure stop and stand over him. He sees an arm raised high. He sees it descend, and he closes his eyes.

Chapter One

A stack of boxes, logoed with the name of a removal firm, formed an untidy pyramid in the centre of Detective Inspector Callum MacLean's sitting room. He referenced a sheet of paper, comparing the information on it with the black marker pen number on every box.

He had a few days off for the move. It had taken nearly three years to get planning approval and complete the construction of his upside-down house, so he was in no real hurry to tackle the unpacking. He placed the list on top of the boxes and paused to admire the view. His new home's floor-to-ceiling sliding doors looked out across the open heath of the New Forest. The heather rolled away into the distance, fold after fold of ancient landscape that faded to a grey streak on the far horizon. The January sun was trying its best to stay awake, but the stars were already high in the sky and a thin moon had risen, pressing down to overwhelm the light, turning the windows into mirrors. They reflected the image of a tall man whose long, dark hair fell over his shoulders. Callum turned away abruptly when his mobile began to vibrate across the kitchen work surface.

'Sorry, sir. I know you're supposed to be on leave. It's Daisy.'

'Problems?' Sergeant Donaldson wouldn't call him unless it was important.

''Fraid so. I was at a meeting in Godshill Village Hall this evening about this summer's gymkhana.'

He could tell she was moving around, there were voices in the background, the guttural growl of some slow-moving traffic and the crisp crunch of gravel beneath her feet.

'It's just ended. The car park's packed and everyone is keen to get home or over to the pub. Someone's been run over.'

Callum glanced around the kitchen to locate his car keys and tried to remember where Godshill Village Hall was situated.

'There's something not quite right about it all,' Daisy said. 'I think you need to see it, Callum. Martha's on her way. The man is dead.'

* * *

Godshill Village Hall car park was lit by a bright, motion-sensor light set high on the top of a pole. Additional police lights cast strong beams from the opposite direction, and the resulting shadows of people resembled giant spiders crawling around in the cold.

Callum walked across the gravel towards the action, his outgoing breath hovering ahead of him, visible in the crisp air. Somewhere close by, a dog was barking, a relentless and noisy objection to the unaccustomed activity perhaps. A man shouted a curt command and the dog fell silent.

'Martha?' He stopped close to the crime-scene-suited figure who knelt beside the body.

'MacLean.' Dr Matha Jones didn't look up and continued to concentrate on her task. 'Yes, he's dead, yes, he's been run over and yes, I'm so bloody cold I could be confused with him.'

Callum slid the zipper of his jacket up another notch.

'You'd think,' Martha continued, 'that my generous covering of flesh would afford me better insulation.'

She nodded her head towards a nearly new Ranger Raptor untidily parked close to the body. 'He was under that when I arrived. The woman driving apparently didn't see him behind her and reversed straight over him. He's a bit of a mess.'

The truck had wide tyres, with deep tread. "H KINGMAN – MASTER BUTCHER" was emblazoned in gold across the tailgate.

'How and when did it get over there if he was underneath it?' Callum said. 'Tell me she didn't drive back over him.'

Martha glanced up at him, and he thought she was smiling behind her mask. 'Much more impressive than that. Six burly young men lifted the back of the pickup and swivelled it sideways up and over the body. They thought he might be saved at that stage. But with his chest caved in like that, there was no chance.'

The front wheels of the vehicle had dragged a ridge of gravel next to each tyre, confirming her observation.

'Heavy vehicle,' Callum said. 'Didn't anyone hear him shout?'

'That's your job. Daisy thought there was something off about the whole thing and I'm inclined to agree with her. She sent everyone back to the hall, so you can go and ask her about it. Now I hope to get the autopsy done tomorrow, but I've got a bit of a backlog. Time of year, MacLean,' she added when he drew breath to comment.

Callum looked more thoroughly at the body. It was a white male, mid to late fifties with a lean face and an unmarked complexion. He was clean-shaven with a full head of hair that Callum thought had been probably grey before it had been dyed blond and made to stand jauntily upright. He was dressed in tight-fitting black jeans, a black puffer jacket and lace-up ankle boots, and Callum's first reaction was that his outfit would have been more suited to a man half his age. Midlife crisis? Callum noted that he wore no wedding band, but his ring finger had a deep furrow encircling it. Recently divorced?

'Right, that's me done here.' Martha extended a hand towards Callum, and he supported her arm to assist her as she struggled to her feet. She exhaled a cloudy breath. 'This weather brings out my inner dragon.' She picked up her case. 'Daisy has his ID.' Her suit rustled as she indicated to her assistant that they could move the body. 'I'll be in touch, MacLean.'

* * *

Inside the village hall it was warm, noisy as a chicken house, and the smell of radiator-cooked dust hung in the air. The naked bulbs suspended from the high ceiling threw pools of yellow light on the groups of people standing talking. Callum paused inside the door to get his bearings. A moment of stillness and silence preceded a burst of comments and activity as they acknowledged his arrival. Many of those in attendance were children and he supposed the gymkhana was being run largely for their benefit. He spotted his sergeant, Daisy Donaldson, on the far side of the room, her slight frame and plaited blonde hair easily deceiving the unaware into thinking that she was still a child herself. Like most of the young people in the hall, she wore jeans, boots and a zip-up fleece. She was speaking to Jimmy Eastwood, the agister. He took his job of being responsible for the stock that roamed wild in his area of the New Forest very seriously and Callum wondered what they were discussing so earnestly.

She looked up as he approached. 'Sir, Martha is with the body.'

'I've seen her. Have you got his ID?'

She nodded. 'I'll have a think about the pony,' she said to Jimmy, who raised a farewell hand to Callum and moved away.

'Right, sir. Our victim is Brendan Stafford, and according to his driving licence, he's not local. He comes from Birmingham.'

'Who was driving the pickup?' Callum asked.

Daisy pointed to a couple who sat together in silence on nearby chairs. 'That's Irene Kingman and beside her is her husband, Harry. They own a butcher's shop in Fordingbridge. She was driving and he's not very happy about being asked to wait for you.'

'Too bad.' Callum studied the pair of them. Harry was probably in his sixties. He had a large frame that he had done his best to fill, judging by the stretched pattern on the front of his jumper. His cheeks were red-veined and saggy, and he had more than the required number of chins. He breathed through his open mouth, his tongue constantly flicking over his lips. Callum's first impression was that Harry demanded and took up a lot of space. In contrast, his wife was almost invisible. She had permed grey hair, and wore stout shoes, a tweed skirt and a twin set, all in some variation of grey.

'I think she was driving because he had one or two in the Drunken Donkey before the meeting,' Daisy said. 'That's the pub opposite this hall.'

Callum had noticed it when he arrived. It was literally across the road from the village hall and Callum wondered why Harry and Irene had not left their vehicle in the pub car park and walked the short distance to the meeting. The butcher did not look as if he enjoyed exercise, so perhaps that was the reason.

As Callum watched, Harry lifted his arm, looked pointedly at his wristwatch before staring across the hall at the detectives.

'He seems keen to get away from here, Daisy. Did he know the deceased man?'

'He said he had never seen him before in his life, and you'll like this, he told Irene that she didn't know him either. She might as well have been a mute.' Daisy's displeasure was clear from her tone.

'It's gone ten,' Callum said. 'I want to get these kids out of here as soon as possible. Get the name and contact details of everybody here and then send them home, except Harry and Irene.' He made to move away, but her next comment stopped him.

'See the woman by the door? Blonde hair with streaks, tied back in a low ponytail? The four girls with her are her daughters and the chap behind them is her husband, George.'

She was easy to pick out. The two older girls were identical to one another and a few inches taller than their mother. Twins? The two younger girls were copies of the older ones. There could be no doubt they were sisters. They each had long, straight golden hair and were of the same athletic build as one another and their mother. The only visible difference was that the shortest one of the four, whom Callum took to be the youngest, wore glasses. The man behind them seemed older than his wife and Callum might have thought him a grandparent if Daisy hadn't primed him about their relationship. Perhaps thinning hair and a lined face were the result of living in a house with five females.

'And?'

'And she is Abigail Garland, the show secretary. She got everybody to sign in and put down their mobile numbers as they came through the door.'

Callum was impressed with the efficiency. 'Get hold of that list and make sure her details are on it. And find out where she lives. We'll go and see her in the morning. Send the rest home.'

'Okay. She runs a bed and breakfast at Crossways Farm. Easy to find, sir.'

Chapter Two

Harry rose to his feet as Callum approached but Irene remained seated.

'Get up, woman, or we'll be here all night.'

With her mouth pursed into a tight knot, Irene stood, her weight evenly balanced on both feet, her shoulder bag clutched to her chest.

'I'm sorry to have kept you waiting, Mr Kingman, Mrs Kingman,' Callum said.

'I can't see the necessity, myself. It was an accident, pure and simple. She didn't know he was there behind her.' Harry's voice increased in volume as he emphasised her lack of blame, and the effort made him slightly breathless. 'They should get better lighting in this damned car park. It's an accident waiting to happen.' The colour rose in his cheeks and his jowls wobbled. 'Right. We'll be off then.' He looked down at his silent wife. 'Get your keys. We'll just make last orders in The Donkey.'

Irene took her keys from her coat pocket without looking at either man.

Callum held out his hand and she dropped them onto his palm. 'Thank you, Mrs Kingman.' He rotated the house keys from the ring and returned them to her.

'Oh, for goodness' sake. How are we supposed to get home now?' Harry blustered.

'Just routine, but we will be keeping your vehicle for a day or two.' Callum ignored the snorted breath from Harry and addressed Irene. 'And you had no idea that the man was behind your vehicle?'

She glanced at Harry before answering. 'The security light is actually quite bright, and the back of the Ranger was in shadow. I walked round the bonnet and opened the driver's door. Harry got in the passenger side.' She paused and looked up at Callum for the first time. Her eyes were as grey as her hair.

'And you didn't see any movement, or hear footsteps on the gravel before you got in your vehicle?'

She shook her head. 'We were practically first out of the door, so there wasn't really anyone else around.'

'Were you in a hurry?' Had they known the man was there and didn't want any witnesses to them running him over?

She slid a sideways look in Harry's direction. 'My husband wanted a drink in The Donkey, and he thought their car park would fill up quickly after the meeting, so *he* was in a hurry.'

Harry drew the bottom of his anorak closed and fumbled trying to fasten the zip which was concealed below the swell of his gut. He tutted with annoyance.

Irene ignored him. 'I started the engine and looked in the side mirrors in case anyone else was reversing out. There were no lights, and I didn't see anybody walking.'

'Or she would have stopped.' The zip growled a protest as Harry yanked it upwards. 'Have you finished with her?'

'Very nearly.' Callum turned his attention back to Irene. 'What noise did you hear?'

She frowned. 'I didn't hear anything except Harry talking and telling me to hurry up.'

'No bang of someone hitting against the tailgate? No one shouted to you? The man didn't call out, or scream for you to stop?' He had noted earlier that the Ranger had reversing cameras and sensors. 'Your vehicle didn't alert you to any movement or obstruction?'

She shook her head slowly as if she was giving it some thought. 'No. I hadn't thought about that. They beep if something moves close to the bumpers. I find it very useful when I'm parking. But I didn't hear any sound. I just felt the bump when I went over him, like driving over those raised bits in the road.' She frowned. 'I'm so very sorry.'

Harry tutted again.

'Did you hear anything, sir?' Callum asked Harry, as Daisy joined them.

'No, I did not. I would have said. And it's his own fault, creeping around the car park in the dark. What was he doing? Stealing fuel or something?'

Callum didn't reply. Now that the hall was nearly empty, he detected the faint smell of raw meat that he associated with butchers' shops. He supposed that if you worked with it all day you probably didn't smell it yourself.

'And did either of you recognise the man? Have you seen him before?'

Harry took a step towards the door. He tugged at his wife's sleeve, and she twisted sideways to slip out of his grip.

'I didn't recognise him, officer,' Irene said.

'Thank you, Mrs Kingman. I understand my officers have breathalysed you and it was a negative result. I will need to speak to you again, but you can go now.'

Callum watched them walk to the door, Harry impatiently chivvying his wife along. He yanked on the handle and, without offering Irene the opportunity to precede him, disappeared out into the car park in a blast of chilled air.

'I think the man might have been lying down behind their pickup, Daisy,' Callum said.

'On a freezing night like this?' She handed him the list made by Abigail Garland. 'Why?' She zipped her fleece up to her chin and thrust her hands into her pockets.

'Good question. He could have had a heart attack on his way to the meeting, some kind of collapse, a diabetic coma or some other medical emergency. I don't think she ran over him intentionally.'

'Neither do I. She was quite shaken but was managing to hold it all together.'

'Agreed.' Callum had noted the slight tremor in Irene's fingers when she had taken her house keys from him.

'And I checked the seat position in the Ranger before you arrived,' Daisy continued, 'and she was definitely driving. There is no way Harry could have got behind the wheel with the seat that far forward.'

That had been his next intended action. She had saved him a few moments in the biting cold.

'Well done. You made a good call. I don't think this is as straightforward as it looks. We'll see what Forensics can get from the vehicle.' He closed the hall door behind them. 'Martha says there might be a bit of a delay with the post-mortem.' Their boots scrunched across the gravel. 'In the morning we'll go and visit the Garlands and see if there is anything they can add. If Abigail was sitting at the door as everyone came in, she might have heard or seen something relevant.'

They walked towards his car. 'Get Cookie to locate the next of kin and ask Bird to go round the local B&Bs and see if he can find out where Brendan Stafford was staying.' Unless the man had recently moved and not updated his driving licence, he had to be a visitor to the area. 'If it is close enough to the hall, he might have walked. If not, he must have a car somewhere. Locate that too.'

Daisy slowed her pace as they reached his vehicle. 'Abigail said she had never seen him before, Callum, so he can't be staying at their B&B.'

'I suppose that was too much to hope for.' He glanced across to the Drunken Donkey where patrons were spilling out into the parking area, their dragon's breath evaporating in the chill air. A couple of young women called goodnight to their friends and crossed to the hall side of the road. Callum wondered if they were coming to see him, or more likely Daisy, but they pulled open the door of an old red phone box that was next to the wooden bus shelter adjacent to the hall.

Daisy marched on the spot. 'It's not really a phone box,' she said. 'It's a mini-library now and when people finish reading a book, they put it on the shelves and swap it for another. Anyone can use it.'

Callum made a note to tell Rain about the repurposed kiosk, although he suspected that his partner might already use the resource. She always seemed to be reading at least two books at the same time.

A car pulled out of the Drunken Donkey. The headlights played across the glass panels that formed the sides of the telephone box, illuminating the two women who emerged, each clutching a book.

A fox barked, the sound slicing through the cold night, an eerie reminder that there were predators out there in the darkness.

'Did he have a mobile on him, Daisy?'

'Nope. None found. I asked them to check the car park in case he dropped it. Night, sir,' Daisy called over her shoulder as she moved towards her Navara and zapped open the door.

Callum started his engine, put on his heated seat and watched her drive away. Reaching up for his seat belt caused Abigail's list to crackle in his pocket. When he got back to Hope Cottage he would check to see if Brendan Stafford had come into the meeting but then left again. If he had, then, although they had not found his mobile phone, they would, at least, have his number recorded. If he had come to the meeting, had he arranged to meet someone there? Or had he come in anticipation of finding someone he was looking for? Callum pulled onto the road. Whatever Brendan's plans had been for that evening, something had gone awry.

Chapter Three

Callum turned onto his driveway and rumbled over the cattle grid, making his headlights bounce up and down. They briefly illuminated the new sign for Hope Cottage that Daisy had given him as a housewarming gift. He had nailed it to a fencing stake and set it beneath the silver birch tree. The gorse bushes in his boundary hedge were glazed with silver and sparkled like tinsel in the moonlight. Two wild New Forest ponies stood side by side, their rumps towards him as they carefully pruned the grey bushes. Their thick winter coats made their silhouettes look as prickly as the gorse.

It had taken him a while to get used to herds of livestock roaming free. When he first came down from Scotland, he had rented a house while this one was being built and, on several occasions, he had omitted to adequately secure his gate, returning home to find ponies in his garden. Evicting them had proved difficult as they seemed to know he was afraid of horses, a fact he had negligently overlooked when accepting this post.

He slotted his key into the door and checked the time on his phone. He had been away longer than he thought. He pushed open the door and the 'pirrip' greeting from his cat, Amber, had him swiftly closing it behind him.

'Sorry, beastie. Daisy said I've got to keep you in for four weeks, so you realise this is our new home and don't go back to the old place.'

Daisy was a local girl and his reliable informant on all things 'animal'.

He flicked on the kitchen lights and immediately saw the handwritten note in the middle of his kitchen table. It had not been there when he had left.

> Cal. You're out! I called in to help unpack your boxes and did a couple. I hope I put the stuff in the right places. Crockery in the drawer opposite the dishwasher and mugs etc. in cupboard above where the kettle will be. I haven't found the kettle yet.

Rain had drawn a frowning emoji-style face.

> Gone home, as I'm on nights until Thurs so will catch up after that. Would have loved to stay and unpack the rest. Rain

A laughing emoji was followed by:

> P.S. Don't struggle to do everything tonight. Take a break and paint a picture or something. R.

The last sentence was written up the side of the paper.

> P.P.S. At least the removal men put all the furniture in the right rooms. That's a bonus. R.

He imagined her smiling as she wrote that. Rain always saw the positives in any situation. He supposed it was a case of opposites attracting. At thirty-six, the rest of the station viewed him as a morose misery. That had been the reputation that he had acquired in Glasgow after his wife

Grace had died, and he was content with that appraisal, doing nothing to dispel their opinions.

Amber wound her tabby body around his legs and purred until he bent down and stroked her. Then she bounded up the pyramid of taped boxes and sat on the top one, washing her face with a sheathed paw. He eased his list out from beneath her and checked the number for the box that contained his kettle. Unable to find it, he began rearranging the boxes into numerical order. This disturbed Amber who made a throaty noise of protest and leapt down onto the floor.

'Some help you are,' Callum said as she climbed into one of Rain's discarded boxes, curled up and went to sleep.

He found the kettle, filled it and switched it on to make coffee. He consulted his list again and located the one containing his sketch pad and pencils.

Moving to the other end of his open-plan house, he sat on the sofa and recorded the date at the top of a new page. He always kept a pictorial diary, a sketch, or a compilation of sketches of what he had done during the day.

He selected a 2B from his tin of pencils and laid a preliminary line on the paper. This habit was a legacy of his first holiday alone with his grandparents on their croft on Seil Island on the west coast of Scotland. Every evening, his grandfather would sit in front of the peat fire and commit his day to a sketch. He had given paper and pencil to Callum who found that drawing a picture was much simpler than trying to write sentences and avoid the words he couldn't spell.

Now, after a few strokes, the image of Rain smiled back at him. He sipped his coffee, inhaled the aroma, and ran a critical eye over the drawing. Callum had just decided to darken the background to better show Rain's pale hair when his phone rang with a FaceTime call.

'Freya.' It was late. 'Is everything okay?'

'Keep the heid. It is, wee man. How's it going? All settled in?' His three older sisters always referred to him in that way.

'Not exactly.' He turned the phone round to show her the stack of boxes; the cat curled into an empty one.

'Amber seems to have found a comfy spot.'

'Indeed. And Rain has been here helping but she's on nights for the next wee while, so I'm on my own.'

'You'll manage. Dolina and Shona gave me loads of instructions to pass on to you, you know our sisters. Most of them boil down to common sense, so I won't bore you.'

'Mum and Dad okay?' He felt a fleeting stab of guilt at leaving them behind, before reminding himself that they had made coping with Grace's death doubly difficult with their constant questions and concern. Moving south had been the right decision for him.

'They're grand, Cal. Send Mam some pics when you get settled in. She bored half the street with pictures of you building the house, so she'll be proud as a peacock to show them the finished result. How are things with you?'

From experience, he knew she was asking how he was coping with widowhood. 'Just fine. Rain suggested that I store things in the nearest drawers to where they'll be used. Crockery opposite the dishwasher, mugs above the kettle.'

'She sounds very practical. I look forward to meeting her when you're ready. Now stop drawing and get on with the unpacking.'

He hadn't shown her that he was sketching and raised a quizzical eyebrow at her.

She laughed. 'You're not the only detective in the family. I saw the end of your pencil.'

Chapter Four

The police station was a brick building on the outskirts of Fordingbridge. It had been constructed on the site of a demolished property that no one had wanted to buy, following the murder of the family that had lived there.

Callum parked and noted that DCI Bertram Bellman's space was occupied. News of the body would have reached him, meaning that Callum would be summoned for an update. Bellman had an aversion to dead bodies littering his patch. A recent spate of domestic burglaries had elicited a rather intrusive level of interest from the DCI and Callum hoped this would be deflected by the death of Brendan Stafford.

When Callum had first come to the station, his relationship with Bellman had been tense and laden with suspicion, caused by the actions of the now-retired inspector that Callum had replaced. Since then, both officers had made an effort to forge an effective working partnership. Over time, Callum had developed a grudging respect for his superior, although he did think that Bellman spent too long chasing targets when he could have been chasing criminals.

Callum pushed open the door to the office. DC Thomas Cooke was seated at his desk. His right hand flashed across his computer keys while his left beat a steady rhythm with his pen against a blue folder. His in-time head movements made his black curls bounce.

'Cookie, where is everybody?'

'Morning, guv. Deedee is making us a coffee and Bird and Legs are going round B&Bs to find out where Brendan Stafford was staying.' Although Callum never referred to his sergeant as Deedee, he was used to the rest of his team doing so.

The outer door opened again, and Daisy reversed into the room carrying a mug in each hand.

'Morning, sir. Do you want me to get you a coffee, too?'

Callum shook his head and turned his attention back to Cookie, who resumed speaking.

'They've taken the photo of Brendan round in person instead of just ringing them, because we don't know if he was using another name.'

'We don't. I checked the list that Abigail made of the attendees at the gymkhana meeting last night and Brendan is not on it,' Callum said. 'But as you say, we can't discount the possibility that he could have been using a different name. How are you getting on with the next of kin?'

Cookie rotated his chair and stopped when it was facing Callum. 'Slo-o-o-ow. It's Saturday and nobody seems to be working.'

'Does he own a car? Index number? Make and model?' Callum said.

'All the vehicles in the hall car park have been accounted for, so he didn't park one there,' Cookie said.

'Good. And check with the nearest police stations to his home address and see if he has been reported missing. We don't yet know what he was doing down here.'

Cookie tapped his pen against his head and said, 'Ping.' He swivelled his chair to face his desk and added, 'Hunky-doodley, guv,' as he reached for his phone.

Callum's gaze lingered on the young detective. The lad had calmed down in the last couple of years, but his internal dynamo was still stuck in overdrive. He still wore black drainpipe trousers, knitted waistcoats and ridiculous ties. Today's was a wide kipper affair that matched his orange socks. His hair seemed to grow at twice the speed of everyone else's and, once again, he needed a haircut. Cookie was an undisputed genius when it came to technology and electronic devices but often impacted the team with his abundance of distracting restless energy and his inability to stand still.

A glassed-off section at the far end of the room resembling a fishbowl was Callum's office. He went inside and sat behind his desk to study the list of people who had attended the gymkhana meeting. Jimmy Eastwood and Daisy, he already knew. Daisy would have attended because of her connection with horses. She had two of her own, and she supported local children's activities. Jimmy was a rider because of his job as an agister; and with four young children, Callum could see why he would attend. The Garlands' offspring presumably had ponies and, if Abigail was prepared to undertake the task of show secretary, she must be keen to ensure that the event went ahead.

The Kingmans were too old to have a young family, and neither looked like a rider, so why had they been at the meeting?

'Daisy, have you got a minute?' Callum called across the office.

She came into the fishbowl and faced him across his desk, her coffee mug in her hand.

He turned the list around so she could read it. 'Who is Keiron Tapper? Why do I know the name Tapper?'

She took a sip of coffee. 'Because he's the thatcher who's been redoing that cottage roof at the bottom of Hatchet Green. He had a sign out on display the whole time he was working there. Green with white writing.

Actually, now I think about it, it says Joe Tapper, because he's still using his dad's old signs.'

He should have remembered. Before he had moved house yesterday, his morning route to the station had taken him past that sign almost every day. He remembered seeing the thatcher standing on a ladder that was leaning against the partially completed roof, lobbing tools down into a red bucket. Hale village had several chocolate-box cottages along its lanes, so Callum had probably seen Keiron many times in the last couple of years.

'He recently took over the business from his dad after Joe was injured falling off a roof,' Daisy continued, 'but his dad is finding it difficult to let go of the reins. Keiron can be a bit bolshy, doesn't care who he offends, but I get on okay with him.'

This was no surprise to Callum. He had not encountered anyone who failed to get along with his sunny sergeant.

'And,' Daisy continued, 'he advertises in the parish magazine, which you get a copy of, so you've probably seen his name in there too.'

He was preparing to point to another name, but she pre-empted him, touching her finger to a line on the paper. 'And she advertises there, too. Penny Hopwood, the hurdle maker. She makes those fencing panels you see, you know, the woven hazel jobs in hedges and gardens. She's building a good reputation because she's pretty good at it.'

He knew Daisy would never have added 'for a woman' as so many still did.

Daisy hitched a jean-clad hip on his desk and pulled the paper closer to her. 'Those are young commoners.' She tapped the names of six men who had signed in one after the other, her booted foot swinging in time to the taps.

Callum realised the word 'commoners' – the descendants of folk who had lived in the New Forest before King William the Conqueror had decreed it his hunting ground – had slipped easily into his vocabulary.

He didn't need her to remind him that their families had inherited Forest Rights, one of those being the right to graze their livestock on the open lawns and heaths. He thought they might be the six burly young men who had impressed Martha the previous evening by lifting the Ranger up and over the body of Brendan Stafford.

Daisy recognised many of the people who had attended the meeting the previous evening and, as Callum had surmised, most had young children who would want to ride at the event.

He was about to suggest that they visit Crossways Farm and ask Abigail Garland for information on the ones they were not familiar with when the outer door opened. DC Almadia Levens strode into the room, her long stride eating up the distance to his door.

'Legs is back,' Daisy said unnecessarily. It was difficult to miss the presence of the tall Nigerian-heritage officer with her penchant for sunset-coloured clothes.

'Morning, guv,' Legs said coming to the doorway of the fishbowl. 'Bird's just on his way up, too.' She took off her coat and unwound the scarf from her neck as she went to her desk.

'Any luck?' he asked, moving into the outer office.

She shook her head, and the ends of her box braids swung around her shoulders. 'Nobody that I visited had any unaccounted-for guests or recognised him from the photo. It's pretty quiet in January generally and some of the bed and breakfasts are closed until Easter when tourism picks up. I asked them anyway; in case he visited and found them closed.' She turned her head away when the door from the corridor opened. 'Here's Bird. Any luck?'

Callum had been curious about the nickname when they were first introduced, as there was nothing bird-like about the officer. It transpired that he and his partner, Helen, cared for injured birds.

'Bingo,' DC Tony Hampton said, unzipping his waxed jacket and draping it over the back of his chair. 'Bleedin' hot in here,' he said, pushing his sweater sleeves up his forearms, revealing military tattoos.

'What did you find out?' Callum asked.

'He was staying with Mrs Olga Brewster at Willow Cottage B&B in Godshill. Checked in six days before he died, so that was last Saturday. He came by car, and didn't book in advance. He told her he was a college lecturer.'

'How long was he planning on staying?' Daisy asked. 'That might give us some idea what he was doing here.'

'I know what he was doing,' Bird said. 'He was looking at houses. There were estate agents' particulars on the table in his room and viewing times scribbled on some of them.'

'That's going to disappoint a seller if he's made an offer and he's broken the chain,' Legs said. She and her wife Gloria had just bought their first home together and they had found it such a frustrating exercise that after they moved in, she said they were never, ever, moving again.

'He told Mrs Brewster that he has family down here,' Bird said, 'but he didn't say who or where. I reckon she was keeping something back, though.'

'I don't know her,' Daisy said. 'What's she like?'

'Little old lady with pink roses everywhere; cushions, carpets, curtains, you name it. Lives on her own and a framed photo on every flat surface.'

'Have a word with the estate agents and see if he told them about a family connection,' Callum said.

'Okay, guv. All the viewings so far seem to be with one agent, a Lucas Norton who works for Ringman & Stoker in Romsey. I'll give him a bell.' Bird pulled his chair back from his desk. 'And I got extra earache from Mrs Brewster's neighbour because the one on one side was burgled last night, and her other neighbour, on the other side, was burgled the night before.'

'Has Mrs Brewster got a dog?' Daisy asked after a moment's thought.

'Yeah. Two. The size of bleedin' Shetland ponies but neither of her neighbours have got dogs.'

'Someone's doing their research because I checked and they're only targeting properties without dogs,' Daisy said. She looked up at Callum. 'You should get a dog, sir. I don't think Amber would be much help at deterring a burglar.'

Callum had to agree with her but didn't respond. Daisy was renowned for knowing all the local livestock by name and dogs always greeted her with open enthusiasm, whatever their usual disposition. She often teased Callum about his wariness of them, and horses.

'What was taken?' Callum asked. Yesterday, DCI Bellman had again grilled him about the local thefts and lamented that nobody had yet been apprehended. His tone had implied that Callum was somehow responsible for this dent in the crime figures. The discovery of a body would undoubtedly take his mind off thieves, for a while.

'Smalls, guv. Jewellery, cash, silver, that sort of thing. Stuff that's easy to nick and conceal and easy to dispose of.'

'Okay. Keep an eye on the burglaries but let's focus on Brendan for now. Bird, make arrangements to go and see Lucas Norton at Ringman & Stoker and Daisy and I will go and see the Garlands at Crossways Farm.' It was too soon to chase up the forensics on the Ford Ranger, so he would leave a second encounter with the Kingmans until he had a clearer picture of what had happened.

Chapter Five

Crossways Farm was accessed over a cattle grid, down a gravel lane from Roger Penny Way, on the opposite side of the road from the Drunken Donkey pub. The B&B sign was visible as they approached, attached to the knurled bark of a silver birch trunk. Daisy drove across the cattle grid and onto the track. The tall hedges on both sides were neatly trimmed and the brown beech leaves that still clung to the twigs were iced with hoar frost.

'Looks well-maintained, don't you think?' Daisy said as she drove her Navara slowly down the slight incline.

Callum didn't respond. He was used to her couching her observations as rhetorical questions and not expecting a reply. The hedge on their left gave way to a large cobblestone yard with a line of loose boxes below it and a house above. The track itself continued along the line of the right-side hedge and disappeared behind the tall paling fence that backed the wooden stables. Callum wondered what was further down that roadway.

Parked in the yard close to the house was a recently plated black Jeep Wrangler, a Land Rover Defender, a tiny light-blue Fiat with L-plates on it, and a smart-looking camper van. A small wooden booth close to the house had a hand-painted sign on the side advertising free-range eggs.

Callum glimpsed egg boxes and an honesty jar inside it. Daisy parked next to the van. A man's head peered around the swiftly opened side door then withdrew as it was snapped shut. Daisy pulled on her handbrake and looked at the closed door.

'Something I said?'

Callum frowned. 'I didn't see him at the meeting last night. They must have guests staying.'

'They are a B&B.' Daisy got out of her cab and walked around the bonnet to join Callum. 'That is what you call a house, isn't it?' She looked up at the dwelling, with its glass bi-fold doors and decking surround. It looked well able to accommodate six people and guests, with room to spare.

A whinny from the stables had Daisy turning to check on the source of the greeting. Abigail Garland came out of a loose box carrying a black rubber skip half full of horse dung. She was accompanied by two Italian greyhounds, each wearing a snug-fitting jacket, one printed with the coat of a tiger, the other with a leopard.

'Awhh. Cute,' Daisy said quietly, then raised her voice. 'Hello, again,' she called to Abigail, who flicked the bolts closed on the stable door and lowered the skip to the ground.

As Callum had expected, both the dogs bounded across the cobblestones to greet Daisy who fussed their bony heads. Their whip-like tails swished from side to side.

He followed Daisy and the dogs across the yard. It was the first time he had seen Abigail in daylight. He introduced himself, thinking that in the bright sunlight, she looked older than she had in the village hall. But, unless her husband looked younger in the cold light of day, he was still considerably older than her. Her shoulders were high and tight. She seemed nervous, twisting her gloved hands together.

Straw rustled and the head of a grey horse appeared over the half-door Abigail had just closed. Daisy moved forward, reached out her hand and rubbed the horse's face.

'I've got a grey at home, too. Moses. He's a devil to keep clean in all this mud, even though he's rugged up out in the field.'

The tight lines on Abigail's face softened and her shoulders relaxed. Callum could always rely on Daisy to break the ice. She was very good at chatting to people, finding the right words to fill awkward silences, the words that would put them at ease. He moved closer to the women, the smell of horse dung from the skip filling his nostrils as he handed Abigail a sheet of paper.

'Your list from last night returned, Mrs Garland. Thank you for lending it to me. It was very helpful.'

She slipped her hands out of her gloves, clamped them under her armpit and folded the paper into her jacket pocket. 'You're welcome. Have you discovered who he is, yet?'

'We're working on that,' Callum replied smoothly. 'You didn't recognise him?'

'We thought he might have come here looking for a room,' Daisy added quickly, and Callum knew that she too had noticed Abigail's sudden wariness.

'No, he didn't. And anyway, I've already got a couple of guests staying. The Palmer brothers. They're birdwatchers, looking for winter migrants passing through.'

Daisy shivered theatrically. 'Cold time of year to be sitting still waiting for a bird to fly past. I think I'll stick to horses.'

Abigail slipped her hands back into her gloves and lifted her head, turning it slightly as if listening. 'Here come the girls.'

Callum couldn't hear anything other than the cawing of rooks in the leafless trees behind the stables, but the dogs cocked their ears.

'It's nice that they all ride together,' Daisy said. 'I've seen them out a few times and they look out for each other. They wait for the little pony to catch up after a canter.'

Abigail laughed. 'That's Flissa on Dumpling. They've all learnt on him but even Flissa has outgrown him now. I'm keeping an eye out for something about 13.2, 14 hands. I asked Jimmy Eastwood last night if he knows of something suitable for sale locally.'

Callum realised that he had come in on the tail end of Jimmy discussing the matter with Daisy on the previous evening when he had joined them in the hall.

It was not until the girls were nearly back in the yard that Callum heard their voices and the crisp sounds of hooves on gravel when they rode around the end of the paling fence. The air was filled with the smell of hot sweaty ponies. The girls dismounted, pulled the reins over their ponies' heads and ran the stirrups up the leathers. One girl, leading her bay pony, walked between her mother and the front of the boxes, heading towards the door of the stable adjacent to the grey horse. She unfastened the drop noseband and throat lash as she walked, and her pony blew air noisily through its nostrils. The other three girls skirted around the adults, the shod hooves of their mounts clattering on the cobblestones.

'This is a picture of the man.' Callum handed a photo to Abigail. 'Do you remember seeing him around the village?'

The daughter walking behind Abigail – Callum thought she was one of the twins – glanced over her mother's shoulder before reaching out to open the half-door of a stable. She shot a swift look at her glasses-wearing younger sister before going into the loose box and closing the door behind her.

'Sorry. No.' Abigail passed the picture back to Callum then bent down and fussed the tiger-coated hound.

Abigail's actions were evasive and Callum glanced at Daisy to see if she had picked up on it too, but Daisy was looking at the closed door of the loose box. He turned his attention back to Abigail. 'One last question. Why did the Kingmans attend the meeting?'

Abigail looked up from the dog. 'Harry always donates the cup for the senior showjumping. He says it's cheap advertising.'

Daisy mock-shivered. 'Summer seems a long way away when we're breaking ice on water troughs.'

'It does. George always helps with the planning but a gymkhana takes a lot of organising,' Abigail said. 'We rely heavily on volunteers and always have our first meeting near the beginning of January.'

'Did George know the man?' Callum asked.

Abigail shook her head and looked up to meet Callum's eyes. 'No. George said he had never seen him before in his life.'

'And the thatcher and hurdle maker?' Callum added. 'Why are they on the list?'

'Keiron and Penny rent the bottom barns from my husband.' Abigail nodded to the track behind the paling fence that the girls had just ridden along. 'I sort of twisted their arms to come to the meeting and suggested they each sponsor an event this year. Penny has already said yes. Keiron can be a little difficult, but nothing I can't handle. I'll keep working on him. I'm sure he'll come round.'

With a thump, saddles were hoisted onto the half-doors. Callum heard the ponies blowing through their nostrils, the rustling of straw and the girls talking to their mounts. One pony was noisily gulping water.

'I'm sure you'll win him round,' Daisy said. 'Are your two oldest girls twins?'

Abigail laughed. 'Everybody thinks they are because they are so alike. But Charlie is seventeen as of last week…'

'Hence the Fiat.' Daisy nodded at the blue, L-plated car.

'Exactly. Darcie is sixteen, Ems is fourteen and Flissa is my baby, she's thirteen.'

‘They seem very nice young ladies,’ Callum said drawing the meeting to a close by stepping away from Abigail. He knew that given half a chance, Daisy would have embarked on further conversation about the ponies, and he did not intend to afford her the opportunity.

Abigail raised her hand and waved it towards the house. ‘Tom Palmer,’ she said.

Callum turned in time to see a man wave back to her. Holding onto the rail, he stepped off the decking onto the cobbles and got into the driving seat of the camper van. Callum put him in his early sixties, dressed for the weather with a woolly hat pulled down over his ears and a pair of binoculars hanging around his neck. He wondered if he was retired or just had a week off work. Either way, every man was entitled to his hobby of choice.

* * *

Daisy started her engine but didn’t put her car in gear.

‘Where to now, Callum?’ Her phone rang and she answered it on speaker. ‘Yes, Bird.’

His gruff voice filled the cab. ‘I’ve just got the report on the Kingmans’ Ranger. Two points of interest. First, the sensor alerts had been turned off, so if Brendan walked or crawled behind the pickup, he wouldn’t have triggered it.’

‘Odd thing to turn off a safety feature,’ Callum said.

‘Not really,’ Daisy said. ‘I sometimes turn mine off if I’m manoeuvring in a tight space. The beeping can be distracting. But I put it back on afterwards.’

‘What’s the second point?’ Callum asked.

‘Fingerprints, guv. On the tailgate, side and back wing, they found loads of prints,’ Bird said. ‘Most they couldn’t identify, and of those that they could, they were mostly not on the system.’

‘I’ve seen it parked on that wide bit of pavement outside the front of his shop,’ Daisy said. ‘Lots of people would walk past it. Kids love writing "clean me" in the dust.'

'Some of the prints were kids, so that makes sense. We took the Kingmans' prints for elimination and we got two positive sets that gave us a match on the Police National Computer.' He rustled paper. 'One was a local, Eddie Gilligan.'

'I've not come across him, Bird. What's he on the PNC for?'

'Mostly petty. Drunk and disorderly. Minor stuff, but nothing for the last three years. The other set is more of a surprise though. It's a Percy Snow. He's definitely on the system. I'd never heard of them, but he was part of an East End gang called the Reindeers. They operated in London back in the eighties, armed robbery, that sort of thing. What's he doing down on our patch?'

'Perhaps Harry has been up to London,' Daisy mused. 'I wonder why? I wonder who his friends are?'

'No contact evidence for Brendan on the bodywork?' Callum asked.

'None, guv,' Bird said. 'There was some blood on the bed of the pickup, but it was animal, not human.'

'Thanks, Bird,' Callum said, as Daisy prepared to end the call. 'We'll go and have a word with Harry Kingman now.'

'Okay, guv. I can't meet the estate agent Lucas Norton today because he is visiting his poor old mum. Or so he says. From the background noise and giggling, his mum must be some go-getter. He's ringing me this evening to see when he can fit me in tomorrow. And Martha's catching up with her backlog and hopes to get to your PM later today, after all.'

Chapter Six

Shaftesbury Street in Fordingbridge was narrow with buildings on both sides fronted by a restrictive pavement. This widened as they headed west and saw the butcher's shop sited on the corner at a road junction.

Harry Kingman stood behind his shop counter dressed in a blood-smeared white apron and a straw boater with a red ribbon encircling it. There were many empty spaces in the glass-fronted counter display, most marked by a daub of blood where meat had rested. There was still a tray stacked with venison sausages and one mounded with minced beef, next to a few pre-packed trays of stewing steak. All that remained on the other trays was the dripped blood and a label heading a metal pin that had been stabbed into the relevant product before it had been sold. Callum thought the artificial green plants edging the trays made it look like an empty fish tank.

'Busy day,' Callum said conversationally, nodding at the sparse offerings.

'It's Saturday.' Harry beckoned to Irene, who moved along the back of the counter to join him. Her white coat was pristine. Harry pointed at the empty trays. 'Start clearing up.' He wiped his blood-smeared fingers down the front of his apron and turned his attention to Callum. 'When can I have my Ranger back?'

'Very shortly. But first I have a couple more questions for your wife.' Callum looked at Irene. 'Mrs Kingman, can you tell me why your sensors were deactivated?'

Irene Kingman paused, two trays balanced on her arm, and looked at him. 'Were they? I didn't know. Harry usually drives so I expect he did it.' She reached for another tray but did not look at her husband.

'It's not illegal.' Harry's tone was combative. 'The beeping drives me mad when I'm in a queue of traffic, so I turn it off.' He snatched up another tray and pushed it at Irene.

Callum thought that the sensors would only be activated if you were driving too close to the vehicle in front.

The bell on the door rattled and a cold draft followed a teenage girl into the shop. Her wellington boots were too large for her and her coat too small. She slopped across the floor, holding her coat together with a skinny hand.

Callum glanced at an incoming text. His parcel had been delivered.

'Mum said have you got some sausages, Mr Kingman, please?' She pushed her straggly fringe out of her eyes with her free hand. 'Cheap,' she added.

Harry didn't seem surprised by the request. He took a handful of the venison sausages, bagged them without weighing them and handed them over the counter to the child. 'There you are, Susie.' His meaty fingers patted the back of her hand as she took the package. 'Tell your mum I'll pop in and see her later in the week, there's a good girl.'

Susie wiped the back of her hand against her coat. She glanced at Callum and Daisy, but didn't speak. Her boots slapped against her bare calves as she headed for the door clutching the package to her chest. Irene's mouth puckered disapprovingly as she watched the child leave the shop.

‘When did you last take your Ranger up to London?’ Daisy asked Harry.

He lifted two more trays and loaded them onto the stack Irene held. ‘London? Never. Why would I want to go there?’ He leaned down into the display of nearly empty trays and straightened a line of green plastic foliage.

‘And what dealings do you have with Eddie Gilligan?’ Daisy said.

Callum caught the swift look that Irene shot at Harry. She instantly looked away and took her stack of trays into a back room.

‘Eddie?’ Harry reached into the display and lifted the half-empty tray of minced beef, resting it against his stomach. ‘Is that Frank Gilligan’s son? Tragedy that.’ When neither detective responded, he continued, ‘I hear he’s getting married.’

‘Why would his fingerprints be on the back of your vehicle?’ Callum asked.

‘No mystery to that, Inspector.’

In the back room, Irene clattered a couple of trays onto a hard surface. ‘For God’s sake be careful, woman,’ Harry shouted over his shoulder. ‘Those trays cost good money.’ He turned back to Callum. ‘Eddie buys venison sausages from me. My Ranger is parked outside my shop on the pavement. I expect he put his hand on it on the way in.’

‘Were you aware that parking on the pavement is illegal?’ Callum asked.

‘Completely aware. Irene. Door,’ he shouted.

Irene came out of the back wiping her hands on a cloth and lifted open a flap in the counter. She turned the sign inside the shop door to show “closed” to the outside world.

‘My Ranger is logoed,’ Harry continued, ‘and any fine you give me will be cheaper than paying for advertising. Now is that all?’

Harry and his tray disappeared into the back room, leaving Irene to open the door for them to exit. Callum heard the bolts snick closed behind them.

'Keen to get rid of us, wasn't he?' Daisy said, pulling the zip higher on her fleece as they walked out of the shelter of the doorway and into the bracing breeze that was chilling Shaftesbury Street.

'He's not the most patient man I've come across,' Callum said.

They walked into the car park, where a large, fluffy cat sat on a low wall and watched them pass. 'Remind me to get a tin of cat food,' he added as Daisy zapped open her car.

The cab was still warm, but Daisy started the engine and the heater before fastening her seat belt. 'Did you see the look Irene gave Harry when we mentioned Eddie Gilligan?' she asked, putting the Navara in reverse gear. The sensors beeped as three teenagers crossed behind them.

'Clear,' Callum said, when the group had moved away. He snapped his seat belt closed as she reversed out of the parking space.

'I think,' Daisy said, 'that Harry was worried Irene would tell us something he didn't want us to know and that is why he hurried her out into the back of the shop.'

'Do you now.' The same thought had occurred to Callum.

* * *

Eddie Gilligan's front door was opened by a man with thinning hair and the remains of his lunch dried onto the front of his knitted jumper.

'Yes?' He was soft-spoken, his quiet voice seeming to remove any need for urgency.

Callum made his introductions across the doorstep before he and Daisy were invited into the kitchen.

Miles Samways introduced himself, gestured for them to sit at the table and offered tea. He busied himself filling a kettle and found mugs in the second cupboard that he opened.

Callum glanced around the kitchen. He was curious that Miles did not seem to know his way around the space and was about to comment on the fact when he recognised the blue cover of *The Twelve Steps* on the work surface.

Miles placed filled mugs in front of them, pulled out a chair and sat down. 'You noticed *The Steps*, didn't you?'

Callum nodded. 'Eddie's?'

'Yes, Eddie's,' Miles confirmed.

Callum thought that the pale eyes wanted to ask how he knew about alcoholics and *The Twelve Steps*.

'I need to ask him where he was yesterday evening.'

Miles hesitated. 'I know he would want me to tell you the truth. He called me yesterday, late morning from The Fish pub in Ringwood and I went and collected him and brought him home.'

Callum heard Daisy shift in her chair, and hoped she wasn't going to jump in with some comment. Miles needed to tell them in his own time.

'He has done so well. Three years sober.' Miles clasped both hands around his mug. 'I don't know the details, but he broke off his engagement to his fiancée, Lucy Cozens, the evening before. It was the anniversary of his father committing suicide and Eddie finding his body. The timing was just too much for Eddie. I just wished he had phoned me sooner.'

'But at least he did phone you.'

'He's so disappointed in himself. Eddie's been in bed ever since the doctor left. He wouldn't even speak to his friend Seb when he came to see him. He's a mess, but I think he'll be okay. I've told him that I'll stay as long as he needs me. I know he'd do the same for me.'

'He's lucky to have you.' Callum pushed back his chair and stood up.

‘Didn’t you want to ask him some questions?’

‘You’ve already answered them.’ If Eddie had been incapacitated and in bed since lunchtime on Friday, there was no way he could have been connected to the death of Brendan Stafford on Friday evening.

Chapter Seven

'What did I just miss?' Daisy started her Navara and looked left and right before surging onto the road.

'There was a copy of *The Twelve Steps and Twelve Traditions* on the side. Miles Samways was as sober as a judge–' he paused when Daisy made a noise in her throat '–so it seemed likely that Eddie is a member of Alcoholics Anonymous. I think Miles is too, and he's Eddie's sponsor.'

'Got it. Eddie went on a bender because the lovely Lucy dumped him, and he called Miles for a ride home.'

A muscle ticked in Callum's jaw. 'It's not a subject for levity, Daisy.'

'I know. Dependency must be a hellish situation to find yourself in.' She reached across to the control panel and a blast of warm air blew into the cab. 'I was just trying to lighten the mood.'

'It's an illness and at the moment he's in a bad place.' Callum looked out at the houses that flashed past, some with curtains open and the rooms bright with lights or the cold blue of TV screens. Others were still in darkness. He wondered how many of those inhabitants had an unhealthy relationship with drink.

Daisy turned onto the narrow road that led to Woodgreen. 'We're no further forward in finding out how Brendan got himself run over, are we?'

'No. But check with the staff at The Fish in Ringwood. Confirm that Eddie was collected in the morning, then we can eliminate him.'

Daisy indicated, drove over a cattle grid and pulled into the car park of Woodgreen Community Shop.

'You wanted cat food,' she said when he looked askance. He had forgotten that he had asked her to stop at the shop. She parked close to a little blue Fiat, and as he walked past it, Callum recognised George Garland in the passenger seat, his long legs concertinaed like a grasshopper inside the tiny car.

'Driving practice,' Daisy said, stating the obvious as she followed him into the shop.

Callum found the pet food section and selected a tin with fluffy grey felines on the label. Out of the corner of his eye he saw Daisy, a packet of biscuits in her hand, at the till speaking to Charlie Garland. Both the girls paid for their respective purchases and the bell above the door tinkled as they went outside together. Callum picked up an additional small and expensive foil tin with a sleek blue-eyed cat on the lid.

'Have you got a cat?' the young girl behind the counter asked as he tapped his credit card against the terminal she held out towards him.

'No, but I couldn't find the elephant food,' he joked, and the girl giggled.

Daisy was sitting in her vehicle with the engine running when he slid onto the passenger seat.

'Brave man.' She nodded at the expensive treat tin and grinned. 'Once she's been fed that, she'll probably turn her nose up at the cheap tins.'

He hadn't thought of that.

Daisy smiled as she bounced the car over the cattle grid and pulled out onto the road heading for Fordingbridge.

'Charlie told me she recognised the man.' Daisy slowed to drive past ponies grazing on the verge. 'I thought there was a reason she looked at her little sister when she saw that picture of Brendan over Abigail's shoulder.'

'That reason being?' Callum said.

'That Charlie and Flissa saw him standing in the yard a couple of days ago.'

'And Abigail didn't tell us this because?' Callum asked.

'Because she didn't know,' Daisy said. 'The girls didn't tell her. Charlie said that her mother is a worrier, lives on her nerves and tends to panic, so they decided not to tell her because he wasn't actually doing anything. Abigail's also a bit paranoid about security. She's always going out to check that the chickens have been shut in at night and the tack room is locked properly.'

Her comments confirmed Callum's own opinion of Abigail. 'Did Brendan tell the girls what he was doing there?'

Daisy shook her head. 'He didn't say a word. He smiled at them and walked off up the track towards the road. The girls thought he had probably got a bit lost walking across the forest and thought that the gate they ride through to get home was public access when in fact it's private and kept locked. They think he must have climbed over it.'

'That's possible, that he got lost, if he doesn't know his way around.' When he had first moved down to the New Forest and began exploring the extensive heaths and lawns, Callum had occasionally misjudged how far he had run and found himself in an unfamiliar setting. It was easily done when one acre of heather looked much the same as another.

* * *

Callum unlocked his front door. He held it open with his foot to pick up the box on his doorstep and carried it, along with his takeaway supper, inside. The parcel was larger than he thought. He hoped he had ordered the correct product.

Amber was lying on the leather sofa.

'Busy day?' He fussed the cat and put his supper in the microwave to heat up. Even the short time it had spent in his car had reduced the temperature beyond palatability.

He fed the cat and brewed a cup of tea before decanting his meal onto a plate and taking it down to the far end of the open-plan room. The TV remote was on the floor. Reaching down to retrieve it, he saw Rain's knitting beneath the table. The blue and green strands of yarn were tangled around each other and the legs of the table like twined vegetation.

'I see you have been busy,' he said to the cat. He decided to eat his supper before attempting to unravel the tangled mess.

He hoped all the stitches were still on the circular needle because whilst Rain could knit, watch TV and converse at the same time, he had no idea how to reestablish the status quo. When he had finished his task to the best of his limited ability, he put the half-formed garment – he assumed it was a garment – inside a carrier bag and knotted the handles together. He turned his attention to his parcel.

The instructions were a single sheet of paper covered in illustrations, and they made no sense. After his first unsuccessful attempt at construction, he surveyed the results and wished he had studied engineering at university rather than art history. Following his third attempt he had a fully constructed, stable, and not unattractive cat climber, complete with dangling attachments, scratching posts and a sleeping hammock. It should help in keeping Amber entertained while being confined to the house.

'What do you think?' he asked, looking around for the cat. She was curled up asleep in the empty box he had discarded.

He poured himself a whisky, stopping after two thin fingers' worth as he thought about Miles and Eddie. It seemed unfair that some people sailed through life with hardly any interruption to their goals while others were confronted by challenge after challenge. He was transported to Seil Island, standing with his grandfather above the sea loch, tasting the salt-heavy air, the heather scratching against his boots.

'What doesn't kill you makes you stronger, lad,' the old man had said, before whistling up his dog and turning back towards the cottage. Now, after all this time, Callum had no idea what had been bothering him on that summer holiday stay, so he supposed it had made him stronger. It was losing Grace that had nearly killed him.

He took a photo of the completed cat climber on his phone and sent it to Rain. She messaged him back straight away.

> On a break. Looks very proficient. Lost my knitting. At yours?

He sent her a photo of the knitting in the carrier bag, and she replied with a thumbs-up emoji.

He settled down to watch the television and add to his pictorial diary. He began a sketch of the four vehicles parked side by side on Abigail Garland's cobblestoned yard. It was an exercise in perspective, and he had just marked in the vanishing point when his phone rang.

'MacLean, I've just done your PM.'

Callum checked the time. Martha was working late. 'Thank you for that.' If she was ringing him at home rather than sending her report to his office in the morning, she had found something significant. 'What can you tell me?'

'He was definitely run over.' She paused and he heard running water in the background. 'Two ruddy great tyre impressions and related chest injuries. Crushed legs. Perfect match for the Ranger axle width. Not much doubt about that. Now this is where it gets interesting. There are no signs of percussion to the upper body commensurate with him being struck by a vehicle.'

He heard her speak to an assistant, telling them to put something away. So far, she had told him nothing that he did not already suspect. Brendan was laying on the ground behind her vehicle when Irene Kingman reversed over him.

'Sorry about that. Where was I?' she said.

'About to tell me why he let someone drive over him without getting out of the way. Did he have a heart attack?'

'Nothing so mundane. He had suffered a massive internal haemorrhage that lowered his blood pressure to a catastrophic level causing a loss of consciousness and organ failure. His heart stopped. Technically, he died of hypoxia via exsanguination.'

'He was dead before he was run over?' Callum said.

'Exactly so. Well dead, and that's why he didn't get out of the way.'

Amber climbed out of the box and sat in front of him on the coffee table. If the blood loss had been due to natural causes, then Martha wouldn't have called him. He tickled the cat under her chin and considered alternatives. Guns and knives were designed to cause blood loss, but there had been no sign of a gunshot wound. He heard Martha open a door and click on a light.

'Are you still there, MacLean?' A chair squeaked as she sat.

'So, he was stabbed,' Callum said.

'Very good. He was stabbed in the back between the ninth and tenth ribs. Single blow. Direct hit into the liver.'

'Odd that he didn't seek help.' A stab to the liver was always fatal unless it received immediate treatment.

'Agreed. It was a small entry puncture wound and before you ask, I haven't been able to identify the weapon yet. We're comparing it with the database. It just slipped between the ribs and the damage was inside his body. The entry wound was practically closed over with no visible blood loss or we might have noticed it at the scene. To the victim it could have just felt like a punch; he might not have realised that he had been stabbed. Another thing, MacLean. He wasn't stabbed through his jacket, just his sweatshirt and tee.' Her mouse clicked in the background. 'And probably leading up to that he was beaten, which wouldn't have done him any good in the long run but wasn't likely to kill him.'

'Would he have survived if he hadn't been stabbed?'

'Very likely, MacLean. He had prostate cancer but that did not contribute to his death, and he may, or may not, have been aware of that.'

'I didn't notice any signs of a fight,' Callum said. 'His face was unmarked.'

'That's because it was a professional job and they weren't targeting his face. They were targeting his body and knew exactly where it would hurt the most. You don't see them as much these days, but his assailant, or assailants, used knuckledusters. And nasty ones at that. Quite a distinctive pattern and we should be able to match it, if you can find the assault weapon. But, beating aside, there is no doubt that the stab wound was the cause of death. Your boy was murdered. Time of death, narrow window for a change, between seven thirty and nine on the Friday evening that he died.'

'Thanks, Martha.' Before he had a chance to comment further, the connection was cut.

Chapter Eight

'Brendan Stafford was murdered.'

They gathered around Callum and the atmosphere in the office changed.

'Martha phoned me last night with the results of the PM. Brendan had been severely beaten and had a single stab wound to his back which proved to be his cause of death. Martha is going to get back to us when they have identified the weapon. He was dead before Irene Kingman reversed over him.' He waited for the interested murmuring to subside.

'The prints on Kingman's vehicle look a whole lot more interesting now, guv,' Bird said, hitching his hip on the corner of a desk and folding his arms across his chest.

'There wasn't a mark on his face. I'd never have guessed,' Daisy added.

Callum repeated what Martha had told him about the knuckleduster injuries. 'And time of death she puts at 9 p.m. at the latest, taking into account the outside air temperature.'

'Nobody left the meeting until ten at the earliest according to Abigail,' Daisy said. 'And the Kingmans were the first out of the door. I saw them leave. That means Irene wasn't responsible for killing him.'

'Not with her car, anyway. But we don't know where he was attacked, it could have been inside, or outside,' Legs said.

'Sounds like a pro job to me,' Bird added. He stood up when Daisy handed him a photo of Brendan and he secured the picture to the board.

'Right, what do we know?' Callum asked.

Bird uncapped a marker pen and began to record information. 'Brendan Stafford. Fifty-eight years old,' he said. 'Down here house-hunting. Last known address: Birmingham. Cause of death was a stab wound following, or in conjunction with, what looks like a professional beating.' His pen squealed against the shiny surface.

'There was no blood in the hall car park, and no obvious indications of any assault taking place there,' Daisy said. 'And he wasn't there just before half seven, unless he was hiding, because nobody saw him.'

'If he was dead by nine, perhaps someone drove him there and dumped his body when everyone else was inside the building,' Legs said. 'He can't have walked there by himself, can he?'

'We can't discount it but there are less obvious places to dump a body,' Callum said. 'Martha says he might not have realised he had been stabbed. He might have just thought it was one more punch. He'd suffered a significant beating, and it was delivered by a person, or persons, who knew where to hit him for maximum impact.' He let them consider this for a moment before adding, 'Find out where he was earlier that afternoon. Did anyone speak to him? Did he tell them what he was intending to do? Had he arranged to meet somebody? Is that why he headed for the village hall? Was he threatened by, or had he made a threat to someone he expected to find there?'

'Perhaps he was beaten to get him to do something he didn't want to do,' Legs said.

'Or more likely to get information out of him,' Cookie said, shadow-boxing a couple of jabs. 'But they went too far.'

'Or it's possible that he realised he was in trouble,' Callum said, 'and went to the hall looking for help but collapsed before he could alert anybody.'

'More likely he was hoping to return the favour and beat ten bells out of someone,' Bird muttered.

'But he didn't strike me as much of a fighter,' Callum said. 'He looked soft, hands too clean. More jaw-jaw than war-war, but I might be wrong.'

'A lover not a fighter,' Legs said.

'Then why didn't he just report it to us when he was attacked?' Cookie asked and shadow-boxed another couple of punches.

'Either he knew who did it and that he deserved it, or he was frightened of retaliations. Or both. Either way, something important stopped him,' Daisy said.

'Like being dead. Okay, I get that,' Cookie said. 'But why wait until he was nearly dead before trying to get help?' He fidgeted from foot to foot.

'His blood loss was internal,' Callum said. 'Martha said he might not have realised that anything was wrong until he felt faint and disorientated. He could have had pain in his right shoulder but that would more than likely be overridden by the severity of the beating. She also said he would bleed out in less than an hour. If he died between seven thirty and nine, then he was attacked between six thirty and eight.'

'So, he was a walking corpse,' Bird said, 'but he didn't know it, and that means he could have been attacked before the meeting in the hall even started.'

'Treat that as the likeliest scenario.' Callum watched Cookie slide back to his desk before turning back to Bird.

'Wilco, guv,' Bird replied. 'I've got a meeting with Lucas Norton from the estate agents later this morning. He's playing in a four at Bramshaw Golf Club. He's told me his tee-off time, and I'm not to be late unless I want to walk round eighteen holes to find him. And I bleedin' don't.'

'If you don't get what we need from Lucas,' Callum said, 'it might be worth having a word with the owners of the properties that he viewed. If he spoke to them, he might have mentioned a family connection.'

'Good call,' Bird said.

Callum looked across the office until he located the nodding black curls. 'Cookie, have you traced his next of kin, yet?'

'Onto it, guv. And we have four more reported break-ins from last night and I'm just trying to get an update on what's missing.' Cookie swirled his mouse at breakneck speed across his desk. 'And nobody has reported him missing – Brendan, I mean – either here or in Birmingham.'

'And his car?' Callum said.

'Still looking for that. It's an Audi R8 Quattro, 71 plate petrol in bright blue. Traffic are onto it. It shouldn't take too long to find.' Cookie was a glass-half-full individual.

'Doesn't stint himself then,' Bird said. 'That's about a hundred grand's worth, second hand.'

Callum thought about the myriad of small gravel areas tucked away down narrow tracks, in dips and behind the cover of trees and gorse bushes. Even a bright-blue flashy car might not be that easy to find.

* * *

Callum's phone rang and he checked the caller display before answering.

'Good morning, sir.'

'MacLean. Tell me about this body.'

Callum could hear DCI Bellman's breaths against his ear. He relayed the scant information they had so far.

'Are you're telling me that he died on Friday, and you are only now upgrading it to a murder inquiry two days later?'

Callum did a speedy calculation in his head. Martha had confirmed the cause of death twenty-four hours after Brendan was found, so it was hardly two days, but he let it pass. 'That's correct. I received the PM report late last night, at home, and what initially looked like an accident turns out to be murder, sir.'

'Have you considered that his death could be related to these burglaries? Is that why he was killed?'

'That's unlikely, sir. There have been four more since the discovery of the body.'

'Four! Are you making any progress, MacLean? If there have been four more, you are letting this get out of hand. What are you doing about it?'

'We are checking for CCTV and cameras, but nothing so far.' He remembered Daisy's comments about him needing to get a dog as a deterrent. 'We seem to have established that they are targeting houses that don't have dogs, so they have been doing their research.'

'Keep in mind that they may be local then.'

'Thank you, sir. The thought had occurred. We found no ANPR hits for unusual vehicle movements that correlated with the dates of the offences. We are already concentrating on a local connection.' Callum was aware that an out-of-area vehicle might have circumvented the automatic number plate recognition system but thought it unlikely. Time was money to a busy criminal.

'Will that be all, sir?'

'For now. Just get on top of these burglaries and keep me informed about your murder.'

'Of course. Thank you, sir.' Callum was about to end the call when Bellman continued speaking.

'I hear you have moved into your new house,' Bellman said. 'I hope it is to your liking, Inspector.'

Callum sucked in a breath and expelled it slowly. 'Yes, that's correct. I moved in on Friday and it's very much to my liking, thank you, sir.' At least he hoped it would be if he ever got to see it in daylight this side of Easter.

Chapter Nine

Legs and Daisy were both speaking on their phones when Callum came out of his office. He went to stand beside Cookie who looked up at him with a brief smile.

'Anything?' Callum asked, purposefully ignoring the pen that Cookie tapped against his mouse mat.

'Good timing, guv. I'm still searching for Brendan's next of kin, but I've just been looking at some footage from the neighbour's door-cam for one of yesterday's burglaries.'

'Who was the victim and when did it happen?' Callum's eyes were snagged by the bouncing pen.

'She's a Mrs Ruby Dixon and it was late afternoon on Saturday when it was just getting dark,' Cookie said.

'What does the footage show?'

'Two youths coming out of the end of Mrs Dixon's drive and running onto the pavement. There's a girl and a younger boy that she pulls along behind her as they run away. She has something clutched in her free hand.'

'Which is?' Callum asked.

'I'm not really sure.'

'Show me, please,' Callum said.

Cookie wriggled in his chair, replayed the clip and leaned forward to get closer to the screen. 'There.' Cookie pointed with his pen. 'I can only get a glimpse before they dash between the back of a white car and the front of what looks like a van and then they disappear across the road.'

'Play it again. Slowly, Cookie.' Callum bent forward as Cookie's mouse clicked, and images flashed across his screen.

'Watch, guv.'

It took just a few seconds for Callum to recognise Susie who had come into Kingman's shop requesting cheap sausages earlier that Saturday afternoon. He didn't recognise the lad she had in tow, but assumed it was a sibling. Neither could he determine what she clutched in her right hand. But it was definitely something.

'Well done, Cookie,' Callum said. 'See if you can pick them up anywhere else and get a better view of what she's carrying. And push on with Brendan's next of kin as your priority.'

'Okey-dokey.'

Was the ill-dressed girl a possible burglar? Callum went into the fishbowl and sat behind his desk. He found the list of items missing after the burglaries and refreshed his memory of what had been taken. All the items taken were both small and valuable. They had ignored any run-of-the-mill items that could be purchased on the high street.

Would Susie have sufficient knowledge at her age to be able to assess the value of the items available? He could understand her taking cash but wasn't convinced that she would steal anything other than money. The cash could be put to immediate use, but how could she dispose of the other valuable items? Susie might be young, but it was no guarantee that she was innocent.

'Sir?' Daisy said from his doorway.

'Come in. What is it?' he asked.

'Bit of a strange call from Jimmy Eastwood.' She slid onto the chair that he pointed to.

'Concerning?' he asked.

'Concerning two girls who were riding their ponies through Pitts Wood Inclosure this lunchtime and were jumping over some ditches and back again. When they leapt over one, one of the girls looked down and there was a deer's head and feet in the bottom. Cue screaming. The other girl got off for a closer look and was paddling about on bloody pine needles.' Daisy rolled her eyes. 'Blood thirsty or what? Anyway, the respective mothers both rang Jimmy and complained about it.'

'And Jimmy is going to let us know what he finds?' Callum asked. 'It sounds like poachers to me.'

'That's what Jimmy said. Did he already ring you?' Daisy pulled a face. 'He's going to ride up there on Pirate and said he'll keep us posted.'

'If it is poachers, then that's one for the Forestry England keeper, not the agister.' Callum had taken a while to realise that as the local agister, Jimmy's responsibility for livestock encompassed the commoners' stock only and not wild animals such as deer. But it wouldn't stop Jimmy being interested in what was happening in his patch of the National Park and Callum knew, that on occasion, the keeper and agister collaborated.

* * *

Bird elbowed the office door closed behind him, shucking his jacket as he walked towards his desk.

'Bleedin' freezing out there.' He dropped the garment over the back of his chair.

'Not too cold for your golfers to turn up?' Daisy asked.

Bird huffed a laugh. 'They filled up with inner insulation at the clubhouse before they started, and all four of them had hip flasks.'

'Better get Traffic to drive past later,' Legs suggested, 'before they run into any Sunday afternoon walkers.'

'Or ponies,' Daisy added.

'What did you find out?' Callum asked, moving to stand beside Bird's desk.

'Couple of interesting things, guv.' Bird rolled back the cuffs of his check shirt. 'Brendan told Lucas Norton he was a cash buyer, recently divorced, and that all the houses down here are overpriced.'

'They probably are compared to Birmingham, but no one in their right mind wants to live in a big city,' Daisy said, then glanced apologetically at Legs who had been raised in Liverpool.

'I liked it there,' Legs said with a grin at her shorter colleague.

'Lucas did *not* like Brendan one little bit. He said the lecturer had a superior attitude and a sense of entitlement,' Bird said, 'which is exactly what I thought about Lucas Norton. Pot calling the kettle if you ask me. Reading between the lines, I think Brendan made Lucas feel a bit inferior, and that would take some doing, believe me.'

'I had a teacher like that,' Cookie interjected, swivelling his chair around to look at Bird. 'He used to spout Latin at us, and we didn't have a scooby until I learned some. Did you know–'

'The solicitor Brendan is using for the conveyancing is from a Salisbury firm, in Castle Street, Waterman and White,' Bird continued, ignoring Cookie. 'I was hoping it would be the same one he used for his divorce. That doesn't look likely. I can't see why he would use a Salisbury firm if he lived in Birmingham, but I'll check tomorrow.'

'Did he say anything about the family he says he has down here?' Callum asked.

Bird shook his head. 'No. But he definitely told Lucas he was moving down here to be closer to them. Lucas was more interested in his flash car. Bit of motor envy going on there. Brendan said he was a retired lecturer at the first viewing, and Lucas looked him up when he got back to the office.'

'And he was,' Cookie interjected. 'I checked.'

'Yeah, he was all right,' Bird said. 'Lucas dug a bit deeper because he had a bee in his bonnet. He says that Brendan took enforced retirement from teaching because of a rumour of inappropriate relationships with young female students. There was an article in the local press, apparently.'

'No prosecution?' Legs asked.

'No,' Bird said. 'But definitely a cloud hanging over him. Check it out, Cookie.'

'Hunky-doodley, Bird.' Cookie swivelled his chair to face his keyboard and began speedily tapping the keys.

'Lucas decided there was no smoke without fire,' Bird continued, 'and concluded that Brendan was a kiddie-fiddler, and he was going to make damn sure he never got to buy any of the houses he showed him. He doesn't want his sort round here. Bit short-sighted, if you ask me. No proof and no sale equals no commission.'

'Couldn't get the educational high ground, so settled for a moral high,' Daisy said.

'I've had a look at his driving record,' Bird said, 'and he might be struggling with a moral high. He only kept his licence last time by pleading livelihood and paying a very hefty fine.'

'They've found it!' Cookie stood up then just as suddenly dropped back down onto his chair. 'It was parked at Godshill cricket pitch. His car,' he added.

'Where's that?' Callum's tone sounded impatient, even to his own ears.

Daisy glanced across at Cookie whose head was now inclined towards his screen. When he appeared to be ignoring Callum and remained silent, she answered Callum herself. 'It's about a half mile along from the Drunken Donkey on Roger Penny Way, but on the other side of the road, and heading away from the village.'

'Walking distance to the hall car park where he was found,' Callum said after ordering the information in his head.

'And to the pub,' Daisy said. 'Why didn't he just leave his car in their car park? Or the hall?'

'Maybe he didn't want it to be seen,' Bird said. 'It's so distinctive, it would stick out like a sore thumb.'

'Perhaps he was up to something dodgy and didn't want anybody to see his car and suspect him of whatever it was,' Daisy said.

'Cookie, get Forensics to retrieve the car,' Callum said. 'Daisy, were his keys with his belongings?' He didn't think Brendan's car keys had been mentioned.

Daisy moved to her desk and shuffled through some loose sheets of paper. 'Now you say it, I don't think they were,' she said. 'Not listed,' she added, straightening up and returning the paper to the heap.

'Right, people.' Callum moved across to the board. 'Get the car park sealed off and get Forensics up there. We still haven't got his mobile phone or his keys. Maybe they are both with his car.'

'It's getting dark, sir,' Daisy said.

'They have lights. Tell them to use them,' Callum said. 'There is every possibility that he was attacked there, so I want it treated as urgent, and as a crime scene.'

'Seems odd,' Bird said, 'that he didn't drive away instead of walking to the hall, especially if he felt rough. I reckon his motor would have been his best hope of getting help.'

'I agree,' Callum said. 'It's the obvious course of action. If that's where he got into a fight and took a beating, one explanation is that he lost his car keys and his mobile in the struggle. Cookie, make sure they have a good look for them.'

'Hunky-doodley, guv.' Cookie reached for his phone. 'They might have stolen his phone. It might have been a robbery.'

'If it was a robbery, Cookie, they'd have taken his wallet,' Daisy said.

'Tomorrow, Bird, get onto the Salisbury solicitor. Confirm that he didn't act for Brendan in his divorce, but ask him what he knows,' Callum said. 'And, Cookie, find me Brendan's ex-wife.'

Chapter Ten

When Callum turned his door key in the lock and pushed open his front door his cat was nowhere to be seen. 'Amber?' He felt a spike of panic. Had he allowed her to slip out unnoticed when he left for work this morning? Was she, as Daisy had predicted, wandering around the village unable to find her way home?

Then he saw her. She was sitting with her back towards him and her head pressed against the closed cat flap. She looked around at him, made a complaining noise in her throat and headbutted the clear plastic. It rattled a protest when she repeated her assault, and her slit-eyed glance at Callum made it clear that the malfunction was his fault.

After supper, Callum settled onto the sofa with his sketch pad and pencil, and a dram of whisky in a heavy crystal glass beside him. He had laid a couple of strokes of graphite on the paper when his phone, which he had left in the kitchen, alerted him to a voicemail. He sensed it was from Rain and wondered why she had not chosen to speak to him in person. He laid his paper and pencil on the coffee table and went to the kitchen to replenish his drink, putting the phone on speaker as he passed it.

'It's me. It's manic here.'

Amber turned her head towards the sound from her position at the cat flap where she had resumed her silent vigil.

'I'll ring you tom–'

A loudspeaker in the background drowned out her next words. 'Adult female trauma ETA two minutes. Two minutes.'

Running footsteps on a hard surface were percussive, ricocheting around the kitchen.

'Coming.'

Then the connection was cancelled at her end. It was difficult to work out what was going on, but Callum assumed that some emergency was on the way into the hospital that had caused them to drop everything and run. Any discontent that he might have felt was kept at bay by the fact that if someone he loved needed urgent medical attention, he would be pleased if the medics dropped everything else and ran to assist.

Amber returned to staring at the cat flap and Callum settled into his sketching, reflecting that both of the females in his life were ignoring him, although for different reasons. He concentrated on his drawing, a landscape of the open heath, the slopes of heather receding to a hazy horizon. He pencilled a stand of squat gorse bushes on the left-hand side, leading the eye into the picture, and a silver birch tree on the right to provide a supporting frame.

He held the picture at arm's length and squinted at it. Then he stood up, leaned the sketch pad against the back of the sofa and walked to the other side of the room to view it from there. He studied it, arms folded, and decided that the drawing lacked focus. It needed something just off centre to hold the attention, something to tell the story.

Returning to the sofa, he sat with his legs along the length of the seating and rested the sketch on his knees. It was quiet in the house, save for the soft skirl of the pencil and Amber's occasional push at her closed escape route. His mind strayed to Rain and her busy night. He wondered about the adult female trauma and his experience offered domestic conflict and drug overdoses. He closed down the memories of past cases and took another, more satisfied look at his completed picture. The foreground was now peopled by a couple with a small child. The little girl was perched on top of a rather rotund pony and her father held the leading rein in his hand. Callum was surprised. He had not been consciously imagining those people and he wondered where they had come from because they were certainly not from his past.

Amber was curled into an ammonite on the mat, and he said goodnight to her as he flicked off the lights and descended the stairs. His bedroom had tall glass doors that opened onto a small sunken terrace. Callum had not drawn the curtains and stood for a moment looking up into the cloudless sky. There was a corona around the moon, hazy concentric rings in pastel shades that obscured its shape, reducing it to a small disc of brightness at the centre. It dimmed the light of the closest stars, pushing them far into the dark depths. It was only when Callum looked further afield from the moon that he could see bright pinpricks of silver glittering in chains above the earth.

* * *

Stepping out of the shower the next morning, Callum saw that he had again missed speaking to Rain, but she had left him another voicemail. He listened to it while he waited for the kettle to boil and worried that she might think he was ignoring her.

'Sorry about running out on you last night. It was all hands on deck.' Her voice was flat, and she didn't sound her usual cheerful self.

Callum wrapped his hands around the hot mug and experienced a sudden urge to fold his arms around her.

'It was a young woman, not much more than a girl really. We threw everything we had at her, but we just couldn't save her.'

Callum heard her sniff a quick breath.

'I ought to be used to it by now, but it gets me every single time.'

She paused to clear her throat, and he dropped slices of bread into the toaster.

'It was a hit-and-run, so your lot have got it now. Poor girl. Don't worry about ringing back. I need to get my head down now. Speak later.'

Callum listened to the message for a second time as he buttered his toast. He typed "Chin up" then deleted it without pressing send. He typed a second response but deleted that too. How could he convey in a few words that he wanted to fold his arms around her, feel the warmth of her body against his, cocoon her in his embrace and tell her that everything would be all right? He settled for "miss you" and pressed send before he could change his mind again.

Chapter Eleven

Daisy drove along Roger Penny Way and indicated to turn off to Godshill cricket pitch car park. Callum lowered his passenger window and held up his warrant card to the constable manning the cordon and they were waved through. A cutting blast of chill air blew into the vehicle.

'Brrrrr.' Daisy gave an exaggerated shiver and raised his window with her driver's controls before switching off the engine. She reached for her jacket from the rear seat and put it on. As soon as her boots touched the gravel, she jogged towards the activity.

Callum stepped out of the Navara. Brendan's Audi had already been removed from the scene and figures were methodically searching the area, pushing aside the prickly gorse and peering down into the bent-over bracken. The dead fronds, glazed with frost, sparkled in the weak lemony sunlight like discarded Christmas decorations. An officer was meticulously breaking the ice on the numerous puddles, presumably checking to see if the missing mobile or keys had been dropped and iced over. Callum took a deep breath. The icy air numbed his chest, and his forehead pulsed with a momentary pain as if he had bitten into cold ice cream.

Daisy had a swift word with the puddle-breaking officer then spoke to another detective.

A half-dozen New Forest ponies stood outside the cordon, some watching the unusual activity within. Their coats were thick, obscuring their bones and trapping warm air. A mare with a hairy moustache carefully nibbled the gorse, manoeuvring her lips to avoid the sharp needles until she had crushed the spikes between her teeth. Callum thought that, with the short turf frozen into a stiff mat, the wild animals had to increase their menu options to survive.

Beyond them, the land fell away into a valley before it rose again in the distance. The browns of dormant heather and copper of the dead bracken on the exposed slopes were starched white this morning and the sky above was a chilled arctic blue. Callum looked up at the call of a wheeling red kite circling overhead in search of his breakfast. Daisy hurried back to him. Her hands were pushed into her pockets and her stride short.

'His car was locked when they took it.' Daisy hunched her shoulders inside her jacket. 'And no initial signs of his keys or mobile, but they haven't finished their search of the area yet. They'll keep us informed.'

Callum realised that this morning's weather conditions, and temperature, were similar to those of Friday evening when Brendan had died. His car would have been his best hope of sanctuary or escape following an attack. He was bothered by the fact that they had found it locked.

His phone vibrated inside his pocket with a message alert, but he postponed reading it. 'Any signs of a fight?' he asked.

The severity of the beating would have left scuff marks in the gravel, or blood on the stones or on the surrounding grass. A barrier of short wooden posts delineated the parking area from the grass of the cricket pitch like a row of shark's teeth. Callum could see that these were being checked for signs of physical impact.

'Not so far,' Daisy said, opening her car door and taking off her jacket. 'But there was an iPad on his passenger seat. As soon as they've checked it for prints, Cookie is going to see what he can find on it.' She threw her jacket into the back of the vehicle and slid into the driver's seat.

Callum joined her in the still-warm cab and checked his messages, but there was nothing that required immediate attention.

'Let's go and have a word with Ruby Dixon,' he said. 'See what she has to say about Susie Treadwell visiting her.'

Daisy's Navara scrunched over the gravel towards the road. Callum could tell from the expression on her face that Daisy was pleased with the prospect of a home visit. She liked visiting houses and said it showed them how people lived. Callum thought that it frequently highlighted things that people would have been wiser to keep hidden.

Daisy turned left onto Roger Penny Way, drove past the pub and indicated to turn right onto the road that wound through Godshill village. Looking out of the passenger window as Daisy drove past the village hall, Callum glimpsed a figure seated inside the adjacent bus shelter.

'Stop. Stop.' He released his seat belt, and the dashboard pinged a protest.

Daisy decelerated sharply and pulled onto the verge. 'What?' she asked, as Callum got out of the Navara.

The bus shelter was a four-sided construction with gaps in the waney-edged board for two windows and a door opening along the facing wall. Callum heard the snick of Daisy's door closing as he reached the front of the structure. Inside, a wooden bench ran along the width of the back wall, and seated on it was a girl, her back leaning against the side wall, her feet up in front of her and an open book on her knees.

'Hello, Susie,' Callum said.

She started and looked up. It was clear that she was so engrossed in her book that she had not been aware of his approach.

'Hello.' Susie put a sliver of paper between the pages to mark her place and closed the book. She brushed her hair out of her eyes with ungloved fingers and frowned at him. 'You were in the butcher's, weren't you?'

'You've got a good memory,' Callum said. 'What are you reading?'

The raincoat she wore today was way too large for her, and she pushed the sleeves up her forearms before turning the book cover towards him. '*The Girl with the Louding Voice*,' she said.

'Any good?' he asked, standing with his shoulder touching the door frame. Daisy caught up with him and leaned in through the window opening.

'Very,' Susie said. 'I'm going to have a louding voice when I'm older.'

Callum wasn't quite sure what she meant and exchanged a quick look with Daisy who shrugged and pulled a 'no idea' face. He knew from Cookie that Susie was thirteen and wondered if her remark was some sort of teenage-speak.

'What do you mean by a louding voice?' he asked.

'I mean that when I walk into a room people will listen, even before I speak.' She made eye contact with him and pulled her jean-clad knees towards her chest. 'Mum… I'm not complaining, mind… but she's caught in the poverty trap and that's not for me. It makes you invisible. But I think you get a choice of how you play the cards you have been dealt.' The sleeves slipped down over her hands and this time she turned back the cuffs revealing a greasy lining. 'The girl in here' – she tapped the book against her knees – 'her mum says education will give her a voice, and she's right. Reading books is free education and I've read nearly all the books in the phone box.'

Callum sensed Daisy swivel her head to look at him, but she didn't speak. Perhaps, like him, she was considering that Cookie might have got Susie's age wrong.

'Why did you become a policeman?' Susie asked.

Her question took him by surprise. He glanced at Daisy as he considered his response and noted that her head was tilted to one side in what he thought of as her information-gathering mode.

'Because I wanted to help people,' he said after a moment's thought.

Susie nodded. 'When I am older, I'm going to be a teacher and help people to learn so they can have a voice, too.' She hugged her arms around her knees, imprisoning the book. 'And then they can all be teachers and help even more people to get a louding voice.'

Callum nodded towards the book. 'You're making a good start, and you're right, knowledge is power.'

'I know.' She studied the book cover. 'People think that because I'm poor, I don't count. They talk at me, not to me, and if they ask a question, I can see they're not interested in my answer. I'm going to change all that.' Susie pushed her fringe back again, her eyes confident.

'I'm interested in your answer to this question,' Callum said. 'Why were you coming out of Mrs Ruby Dixon's house on Saturday, early evening?'

'Uncle Vinny is staying with us, again, so Mum sent me to collect her wages. She likes cash, and Mrs D never has enough to pay her for cleaning. That's why I couldn't pay for the sausages when you saw me in the butcher's on Saturday. Mum cleans for some of the people in the village and they all pay her cash. Mrs D always makes her wait for her money. Mum thinks she does it on purpose. She sent me to get it, and I took Freddie with me. She was out the first two times I went, so I had to go back again, after I went to the butcher's. Why did you want to know?'

'Just routine. Nothing to worry about.' Callum's phone pinged a message and he glanced at the banner across his screen. 'Thanks for your help. We've got to go. Enjoy your reading.'

Chapter Twelve

Once back in the cab, Daisy said, 'There have got to be warmer places to read than a draughty wooden bus shelter with holes in the wall.'

'I agree but perhaps those places don't afford her peace and quiet. With three younger brothers at home and now Uncle Vinny, I imagine it is a noisy household.'

'Probably. What was the message? Where to now?'

'It was Cookie. He has found Brendan's ex-wife. Get him on the phone, please.'

Callum checked his other messages while he waited, but there was nothing more from Rain.

'Hi Deedee.' Cookie's upbeat voice filled the cab.

'You're on speaker,' Daisy cautioned quickly. 'The boss wants to know about Brendan's wife.'

'Hunky-doodley. I found her, guv. Well sort of. I mean I know where she is.'

'Where?' Callum asked.

'When I say I know where she is, I don't mean that I exactly know where she is,' Cookie said cautiously.

'Explain.' Today was not going as well as it might.

'She's called Victoria Josephine Stafford and after the divorce was sorted, she took a holiday, guv. She's currently trekking in the Tortuguero National Park in Costa Rica.'

Cookie spoke Spanish and his pronunciation was full of Iberian flair. 'It's a rainforest and one of the wildest jungle areas you can visit so she's off grid. But I did leave her a message to call you as soon as she can.'

'You can't do more than that,' Callum said. 'Anything else?'

'Yep. But it's a bit weirdy. I've got Brendan's iPad now. It was just his prints on it, by the way. Anyway, I've just started on it. I looked at his photos first and the last ones he took were of Charlotte and Darcie and the other two Garland girls. They were on their ponies and there are quite a few different times that he snapped them, but all recent. There is also a short video too, of them riding across the cricket pitch together – you can see the railings in the background. It was a windy day, so his comments are a bit indistinct. He calls to them–'

'By name?' Callum interrupted.

'No. He just calls "Hello" and they turn their heads to look at him, but they don't answer,' Cookie said. 'The one in front says something to the others that I can't decipher and then they break into a trot and all ride away. The one in front looks back at Brendan just before they follow the track in between the gorse bushes and disappear.'

'Why is that weird?' Callum asked. Calling a greeting seemed like a normal interaction between people meeting in the course of their leisure pursuits. He himself regularly ran on Hale Purlieu and often shared a word with the people he passed.

'That's not the weird bit, guv. He films them riding away and you can hear him say what pretty, and sweet girls they seem. That's what I think is weirdy.'

'Gets my vote for weirdy, too,' Daisy said with an exaggerated shiver.

Callum ignored her. He looked up through the windscreen as a red kite spiralled above them, momentarily blocking out the light and casting a dark shadow into the vehicle. 'Cookie, go back through his search history and see what sites he visits. Check his photos and videos.' Callum heard the rustle of paper followed by the scrape of Cookie's pen. 'Are there other similar attempts to engage those girls, or other girls in conversation? Who else did he photograph? The photos will be dated, so how long has he been doing this and who are his targets? And, Cookie, see what you can find out about an Uncle Vinny who is staying with Susie Treadwell's mother, Janey.'

'Okey-cokey, guv. And they haven't found his phone yet at the cricket pitch, but the photos seem to be from both devices, his iPad and his phone.' Cookie cut the connection.

Daisy started her engine but didn't immediately drive away. 'Do you reckon he's into grooming young girls, Callum?'

'We can't discount that possibility, but it doesn't fit the usual pattern for grooming,' he said. 'Charlie and Darcie are sixteen and seventeen. Targets are usually younger than that.'

'Emilia and Felicity are younger.' Daisy swept the wipers across her windscreen to combat the sudden fall of sleety-looking rain drops. 'But victims are usually less self-assured and less well-off than the Garland girls.' She put her vehicle in gear. 'We'll have to wait and see what Cookie finds, won't we? Where to now?'

'Agreed.' Callum wondered if Cookie would find snaps of Susie Treadwell on the iPad. 'Let's go and visit Ruby Dixon and confirm that Susie isn't our burglar.'

* * *

The Dixons lived in a cul-de-sac where the bungalows lined the approach road and surrounded the turning area with the uniformity of dwellings on a *Monopoly* board. They were all constructed of the same mock stone and pebble-dash facade, and each property had a ceiling-to-floor picture window that overlooked the short concrete drive and pavement. Low walls separated the gardens from the public domain and some householders had individualised their properties by planting a shrub border. The Dixons had elected to build a tall brick pillar on both sides of their drive, each topped by an embarrassed-looking stone eagle.

The detectives stepped across the pavement and onto the concrete. Callum was aware that a woman was watching their approach from inside the large window, partially concealed behind a tassel-edged curtain. All he could ascertain was that she was of medium height and wore trousers and a blouse. She was quick on her feet, though, because she opened her front door before he had an opportunity to lift the brass eagle knocker and bang it against the back plate.

They followed the musky trail of her perfume into the sitting room where every flat surface was covered with nick-nacks and china ornaments. It was busy and unsettling, reminding Callum of a junk shop.

'Do sit,' Ruby said. She swept her arm towards a flower-patterned sofa, and the charms on her heavy silver bracelet chinked against one another.

She perched on a matching armchair, her back very straight and her chin held high. Her hair was short, carefully coiffured but the greyed roots were showing through as if she was trying to eke another week out of the pretence that she was a blonde.

Callum asked her about Susie Treadwell.

'Well, there's a one. She never seems to have any clothes that fit her, and I doubt she's ever seen the inside of a hairdresser's.' She poked a red acrylic nail at her own hair and relaxed back into her chair.

'Her mother works for you, I believe.' Daisy's voice was pleasant, but Callum could tell by the slant of her mouth that she did not feel similarly amenable.

'I was only saying yesterday to my friend Marcia – she runs the book club – that there have to be better cleaners out there. Perhaps one day–'

'So, she does work for you?' Daisy persisted.

'At the moment, yes, she does. She's acceptable as a cleaner but I find that she's such a nuisance because she always wants to be paid in cash, and that's very inconvenient for me. My Reginald is a bank manager, you know, and he says it's ridiculous in this day and age not to have a bank account.'

Callum had already checked out the couple and whilst Reginald did work for a bank, he had not yet aspired to the dizzy heights of manager.

'Have you seen Susie recently?' Callum asked.

'Janey was here on Friday, of course, but I didn't have sufficient cash to pay her, I often don't, so I told her she would have to send Susie round to collect her money on Saturday. As it happens, we were out most of the day, we had luncheon with Reginald's brother and his wife, so heaven knows how many times she had traipsed round here, banging on the door.'

Callum was sure that Ruby had made the arrangement knowing she would be out. A muscle fluttered in his cheek, and he noticed that Daisy flashed a look in his direction.

'I think she only came here once and luckily you were home,' Callum said, and Daisy caught his eye and grinned.

'That's all right then,' Ruby said, but she sounded disappointed. 'The girl ran off up the drive dragging that brother of hers with her – the one that always has a runny nose.' She sniffed her disapproval.

Callum pulled his feet towards him, preparing to stand. He was aware that Uniform already had all the information regarding Ruby's burglary. She had reported that they had stolen some valuable rings that had belonged to her mother, and her 'good' pearls with a ruby clasp. He was not going to let her repeat it all over again. He stood abruptly.

'You'd think Harry Kingman would take Janey in hand, wouldn't you? Four children with four different men, one hesitates to call any of them fathers. And I see that

Vincent is back again. The last time he was here my garden gnomes were stolen.' She looked up at Callum, clearly anticipating a response.

'Why would you think that?' Callum said. He had no idea why Ruby was alluding to a connection between Janey and Harry.

Ruby plucked at, then entwined her fingers in, the string of red and gold beads that drooped between her breasts. 'Because she is the daughter of Harry's dead sister, Pauline.' She sat forward in her chair. 'And I can tell you, reading between the lines, that Irene thinks she is nothing but a liability.' She gave a sharp nod of her head to confirm her comments. 'Reginald says we all make our own life choices, and that nobody should feel responsible for the poor choices of others.' She lifted her chin a fraction, and her mouth puckered into a knot.

Callum had a feeling that Reginald's remark had not been about Janey.

'That's one of the reasons I employ her.' Ruby stood up. 'You have to help those that are so less fortunate than yourself, where you can, don't you?' She flicked an invisible speck from the sleeve of her blouse, smiled at Callum and took a step towards him.

He could smell the heavy scent of her perfume as she inclined her upper body closer to him.

'Between you and me,' she whispered conspiratorially, 'Irene thinks Janey and those kids take advantage of poor Harry's good nature.'

Chapter Thirteen

Walking back along the pavement towards Daisy's vehicle, Callum inhaled the smells of decomposing leaves surrounding a naked tree they passed and chimney smoke that was being pressed earthwards as the temperature dropped with the approach of darkness.

Daisy trotted a couple of strides to keep up with him. 'Ruby's a better detective than me, Callum. Do you reckon you should consider employing her?' She moved out into the road to get to the driver's side of her vehicle and zapped it open.

Callum was used to her rhetorical questions and did not respond. He climbed into the cab and motioned to her to start the engine. The cold was beginning to bite.

Daisy continued speaking as she clicked closed her seat belt. 'You see, I had failed to notice that Harry has a good nature. He must only show it to a very select few.' She indicated and pulled out into a stream of slow-moving traffic.

Callum turned his face towards the window so that Daisy couldn't see that he was amused by her comment. He had similarly thought that Harry kept any semblance of a good nature well hidden. They paused at the traffic lights and his eye flitted over the adjacent houses. Most had lights spilling out onto their gardens as if they were caught unawares by the creeping onset of darkness and had not yet found time to cover their windows. Others had already drawn their curtains so that just a sliver of brightness peeped out into the gloaming.

Daisy's phone rang. She looked at the dashboard screen. 'Jimmy,' she said and pressed accept. 'Yes, Jimmy?'

In the pause before Jimmy spoke, Callum heard the ting of cutlery against crockery, the voices of his four young children in the background and Sue Eastwood telling someone to get their elbows off the table.

'Feeding time at the zoo,' Jimmy's rich baritone announced, and Callum detected the smile in his voice. 'Tell the boss–'

'I'm driving. He's sitting beside me,' Daisy interrupted.

'Good. I rode up to Pitts Wood on Pirate and found what was left of that deer carcass. It was like the girls said, head and hooves. It is poachers.'

'How long has it been dead?' Callum asked.

'Four, five days at least. Something has been eating it, but I could see that it had been shot. A clean headshot; it would have dropped where it stood. He knew what he was doing. He buried the gralloch.'

'The what?'

'Gralloch. Guts, his innards. A good marksman, plumb shot in the middle of the forehead. I've informed Forestry England.'

'Or *she* was,' Daisy said.

'Or *she* was,' Jimmy repeated.

Callum could tell that Jimmy was grinning at Daisy's perpetual reminder about gender equality. 'What sort of weapon?' Callum asked.

'Working on that,' Jimmy said. 'I'll let you know. Got to go, or the vultures will eat my tea.' He ended the call and Daisy's radio filled the sudden silence.

'It's cheap meat,' Daisy said. 'Whatever they tell you, people round here have always poached game, rabbit, pheasant, you name it; it goes with the territory. Even as far back as William the Conqueror, when it cost you your life if you got caught poaching deer.'

Callum thought that was likely. Who was going to pass up a free buffet when food was in short supply back in the day. Mention of meat reminded him that he needed to buy supper for Amber. He had decided against feeding her the expensive tin he had bought in case Daisy was right. 'That's probably true. Can you stop at the shop when we go past, please?'

* * *

Daisy drove over the cattle grid and into the gravel car park of the community shop. 'I'll wait here. I want to check these texts,' she said.

The little blue Fiat was parked against the paling fence, and this time there was no one in the passenger seat. Callum hoped that Charlie had not driven herself down to the shop. He pushed open the door, and saw her ahead of him in the aisle, looking at the magazines. Over the top of the shelves, he saw Abigail passing items for posting over the counter at the other side of the building.

Charlie looked up when he stood beside her, and glanced anxiously towards her mother, then back to Callum.

'Hello,' she said.

'I'm glad I caught you on your own,' Callum said.

She let out a quick breath. 'You want to ask me about something that I haven't told mum. Be quick, then. She's just posting a couple of letters.'

Callum decided that a direct question would be the best way to get a direct answer. 'Did you know that Brendan, the man you saw standing in your yard, had taken pictures of you and your sisters riding your ponies?'

Charlie huffed a breath. 'Creep,' she said. 'It was last week when we rode across the cricket pitch. He called to us, and I told the others to ignore him, and we kept going.'

'Do you know what he wanted?'

'We didn't wait to find out, but I looked back as we rode away, and I saw him taking pictures of us on his phone.' She shivered inside her quilted jacket and flicked a glance in the direction of the counter. 'Don't tell Mum.'

'I won't, unless I absolutely have to.'

Charlie selected a magazine and started to move away, then stopped. 'That's the second time he did that – taking photos when we were riding across the cricket pitch, I mean. We've been going the other way since that last time. At least we can start riding that way again.'

'When was the first time?' Callum asked, then glanced up to check where Abigail was.

'Earlier that same day, when we rode out of our gate onto the track. He was near the gate on the left, so we turned right.'

'Do you know why he was photographing you and your sisters? Did you see him snap anybody else?' Callum asked.

Charlie shook her head. 'No. Just us. The more I think about it, Mr MacLean, the more I think that he wasn't just lost when Flissa and I saw him in our yard.'

'Don't worry about it, Charlie.' Callum glimpsed Abigail moving towards them and looked around at the shelves. 'Can you tell me where cat food is, please?' he asked.

'Next one over,' Abigail said, joining them, and Charlie pointed in that direction.

'Thank you.' Callum moved past them and round the corner into the appropriate aisle.

* * *

The moon lit his way from the lane, through his gate and up the path to his front door. The corona of the previous night was missing but the light was sharp enough to afford him his escorting shadow. In the clear, still air, the sound of a fox yipping and the panicked squawk of a pheasant carried, but Callum could determine neither the distance, nor the direction from which the sounds emanated.

He picked up two envelopes from inside the door, hung up his coat and went into the kitchen.

'Supper, Amber.' He opened a tin, forked half of the contents into a clean bowl, and switched on the oven as he passed it. He put the cat food on the floor, and she ran to him, tail aloft, and rubbed against his legs.

'Forgiven me then?' He ran his hand along her back and up her tail and was rewarded with her throaty purr.

Callum was dishing up his own supper when Rain FaceTimed him. She was wearing her work clothes, and he was relieved to see that she looked like her usual cheerful self.

'I missed you too,' she said, by way of greeting.

'That's all right then.' He held his phone in his left hand and carried it around the kitchen with him, so that he could see her face. He switched off the oven, then lifted out two dishes one at a time and put them on the island.

'What are you having for supper?' she asked. 'I have just eaten the most wholly unhealthy breakfast that you can imagine, but it tasted so good. It was a bit of a night last night, and I think I needed it.'

'What did you have?' He took tongs and then a plate out of drawers and turned back to the island.

'You'll think it was disgusting, but bacon, scrambled eggs, hash browns, beans and sausages.' She grinned at him. 'And chips. I nearly forgot the chips.'

'Truly disgusting,' he said with mock disapproval. He turned his phone around to show her a bowl of salad, then panned across to include the plate of sausages and chips he had just finished cooking in the oven.

You can't eat salad and sausages,' she protested with a laugh. 'It must be the haggis you lot eat up in Scotland. It's ruined your taste buds, Cal.'

Callum didn't like haggis, but he didn't want to spoil the mood by pointing it out.

Chapter Fourteen

'Morning, guv,' Legs said. 'There were two more burglaries last night, both in Hale; that brings us up to nine, but we might have had a stroke of luck at last.'

Callum was already aware that DCI Bellman was waiting for a progress report. He had stopped Callum in the car park on his way up to the office. It seemed that one of Bellman's golfing chums had been burgled and now Callum's superior officer was holding him responsible for the lack of results in apprehending the perpetrators or retrieving any of the stolen goods.

'Which was?' He focused on Legs.

'Which was that an attempted burglary was interrupted by a neighbour on Hatchet Green. The man who was burgled doesn't have any dogs, but his next-door neighbour does, and they frightened off the intruders. They ran away before they had the chance to steal anything. They were trying to get in through a downstairs toilet window.'

While Callum had waited for his own house to be built, he had rented a property alongside the village green.

'Who was the attempted-burglary victim?' he asked.

Legs consulted the sheet of paper she had brought with her. 'A Mr Glynn Roberts at Greenside Cottage.'

Callum recognised the name. Glynn was an elderly widower who lived alone and was hard of hearing. His neighbour with the dogs would be Daphne Smart, the retired headmistress who had two black Labradors that only she and Daisy seemed to be able to tell apart. She had been helpful to him in a previous investigation when a child had gone missing.

'She's been interviewed?'

Legs nodded. 'Yes, guv.'

'What did she see?'

'She said her dogs started making a racket, so she let them out into her back garden, and they went immediately over to the fence that separates her garden from Mr Roberts's next door. The dogs triggered her security light, and she saw two people running away from the house towards Mr Roberts's gate and the road. She thinks one of them might have been injured because they seemed to be limping, and the other one had to help him through the gate.'

'Good. Did she see their vehicle?' They had to have driven away from such a rural location. Daphne still had a sharp mind, despite being elderly, but Callum knew she was not good at recognising car makes in daylight, let alone the dark.

'She thinks it was a tall, delivery-type van – she's a bit hazy on that but she was sure that it had high and low back lights. It drove off towards Woodfalls and all the rear lights were working.'

That was just the sort of thing Daphne would notice. Fleeing the scene in a vehicle ruled out Susie, but not Uncle Vinny.

'Then she went round to check that Glynn was okay,' Legs continued, 'and he was watching TV with the volume turned up so loud that he had no idea what had just happened.'

'Where were the two other burglaries?' Callum asked.

Daisy came through the outer door into the office and stood beside Legs in the doorway of the fishbowl.

'Along Hale Purlieu,' Legs said. She looked round at Daisy. 'Hi, Deedee.'

'You're talking about the burglaries?' Daisy said. 'I was just going to update you, sir. Jewellery and cash taken from two properties along the purlieu.' Most of the properties along that stretch were set well back from the road and a thick belt of rhododendron bushes screened them from passing eyes.

'I already told him about the cottage on the green,' Legs said, and went back to her desk.

Daisy watched her leave. 'I had a quick look at all the local likely bods, but nothing is making a good fit,' Daisy said. 'And, just so you know, Ruby Dixon has been onto the front desk already this morning to ask if you have "apprehended my culprits". The desk sergeant told her she would be the first to hear when we did. He got the impression that she intends to ring in every morning until we get her good pearls back to her.'

'Guv. Guv.' Cookie erupted from his seat and skidded across to Callum's doorway. 'I've got Brendan's wife, I mean ex-wife, on the phone. Will I put her through to you?' He twirled round and headed back to his desk without waiting for a reply.

Daisy shook her head. 'No, Cookie,' she muttered. 'Tell her we are far too busy to talk to her today.' She went back to her desk as Callum's phone rang.

'Detective Chief Inspector MacLean, Victoria Stafford here, phoning you as requested. How may I help you?' Her voice was well modulated and clear, despite the distance between them.

Callum thanked her for calling and corrected her on his rank.

She laughed. 'You probably deserve to be promoted to chief inspector for managing to find me. I'm on a sort of jungle safari in Costa Rica, living in tents and paddling about in canoes, with a guide, of course.'

'It sounds like a unique holiday.'

'My treat to myself for surviving long enough to retire. Now why did you ask me to contact you?'

She took the news of Brendan's death well, but the fact that he had been murdered came as a surprise.

'I was going to ask you if you were sure,' she said, a light tremor in her voice. 'But you wouldn't be telling me if you weren't certain. Poor Brendan.' She cleared her throat. 'I didn't think he knew those sorts of people.'

She asked when he had been killed and when Callum told her said, 'Not guilty, although you probably had me down as your number one suspect, save for the fact that I was over here by then.'

Callum had already checked when she had left the country. 'Why do you say that I should think you the number one suspect?' he asked.

'Because of his affairs. We have – I mean had – been married since we were both students and he had been having these little liaisons practically since our honeymoon. It used to amuse me that he thought I didn't know about them. Everybody knew about them. He was so juvenile.' Her laugh was full of amusement without a trace of bitterness.

'If you don't object to my asking, what changed, that brought about the divorce?'

'When he and his conquests were about the same age, it was somehow more acceptable to me. It seemed like youthful silliness. After all, it was me he came home to.'

Callum thought he heard somebody at her end mention suntan cream, but Victoria didn't respond to them.

'He always thought that he was untouchable,' she continued, 'that his smile was his get-out-of-jail-free card. And it pretty much was until he got involved with the dean's granddaughter. What an idiot.' She took a breath and eased it out slowly. 'There were pictures, you see, and the stink that followed rose to a very high level. He couldn't smile his way out of that one. Suddenly I saw it for what it really was, seedy and obscene and tawdry; his old, saggy body taking advantage of her youth. And all the others through the years. He was nothing but a predator.' Her breath fluttered in her throat. 'I don't know why I never saw it before.'

'And that was why you divorced?' Callum asked.

'No. It wasn't just that. That day, when he came and told me what had happened with the college authorities and that he would have to give up his position, we had a terrible fight. A verbal fight, nothing physical, but I think it was the most emotion that either of us had displayed towards one another in years. He had never changed. It might have been different if we had children, but he was never ready. I wanted them, rather desperately when I realised that time was running out for me. But he kept putting off any decision and coming up with reasons that we should wait a bit longer. And then it was too late.' Her voice dropped and she sounded suddenly weary. He heard unfamiliar bird calls somewhere close to her.

She was silent for so long that Callum wondered if she was regretting sharing her personal information. He was trying to decide if he should prompt her when she continued speaking.

'Anyway, the scales just fell from my eyes, and I never wanted to see him again.' She emitted a tight little laugh. 'And now I never will.'

Brendan had readily agreed to the divorce. They had split the proceeds of the house fifty-fifty, she had kept her pension, and he his. Now he was laying in the mortuary, and she was canoeing around in the jungle.

'Who is the beneficiary of his will?' Callum asked.

'I can't imagine,' Victoria said, 'but I can guarantee that it won't be me.' She told Callum the name of the Birmingham solicitor who had handled the divorce for Brendan and suggested that they might hold his will.

'I wrote a new will before I came here,' she said. 'I didn't want to get eaten by some form of crocodilian and him inherit everything as my named beneficiary. My four nieces share the spoils now, if there is anything left when I go.'

Victoria could shed no light on any relatives in the New Forest. 'He has a cousin somewhere – Elaine, I think her name is. I can't recall her husband's name, Jim, or John, or Jeff, perhaps. The only contact we ever had with them was a card every Christmas. I never actually met them, and I can't be sure, but I think they live in Yorkshire, somewhere on the coast. Brendan wasn't very hot on family ties.' She cleared her throat. 'Or on any sort of family loyalty either, as it happens.'

Callum ended the call with Victoria promising to inform him if she thought of anything that might help him with the investigation into Brendan's death.

Chapter Fifteen

He had barely replaced the receiver when Cookie scooted into the fishbowl. 'Forensics report, guv.' He waved a sheet of paper in the air.

'On what?' Callum said.

'Brendan's Audi.' Cookie's voice registered surprise that anyone would need to ask. 'The only prints inside it are his own. No dings or dents in the paintwork, no signs of a struggle, or similar impact and by the way, they didn't find his keys, or his phone at the cricket pitch or find any signs that there was a fight there either.'

Callum had been reasonably sure that the attack had occurred elsewhere. It was the only thing that made sense. They had eliminated the village hall car park and now the cricket pitch location as the scene of the attack on Brendan.

'Oh, and his satnav,' Cookie said. 'Last destinations he plumbed in, actually all of the local ones, were his bed and breakfast at Willow Cottage with Olga Brewster where he was staying, the houses he viewed with Lucas Norton, the estate agent – they were both in Godshill – and then Crossways Farm B&B. They must be the only places he wanted to be able to get to without getting lost.'

'And all of those were entered after he arrived here?' Callum asked.

'He put Willow Cottage in before he left Birmingham, but the rest were all after he got here, guv.'

'How are you progressing with a timeline for Brendan on the day that he was killed? I need to know where he went that day, who he met, what he did.'

'Sort of nearly there with that. I'm just waiting for a few bits of information.'

'Hurry it up, Cookie. We need the names of all the people he saw that day, because one of them killed him.'

Cookie hurried back to his desk. Callum wondered if the detective did anything at a normal pace, then decided that if Cookie's brain jumped about at hyper-speed, it was not unreasonable that his body would try to keep up.

Sitting back in his chair, Callum pulled a sheet of paper towards him and sketched a pair of cottages, not unlike those belonging to Daphne Smart and Glynn Roberts. Sketching helped him think. He would apprise Bellman of this new information about the burglaries, such as it was, but would have nothing to report about the golf trophy that was of such interest to the detective chief inspector. Callum's team were keeping in close contact with the various local neighbourhood watch coordinators and now there was more information available to share with them, they might get some useful feedback.

What interested Callum was the fact that Brendan had already settled into Olga Brewster's cottage before he visited Crossways Bed and Breakfast. Did he not like his accommodation? Did he not get along with Olga and so was considering moving elsewhere?

Callum looked around the outer office then went to his doorway. 'Legs. Have you got a minute?' he said.

Legs came over to him. 'Yes, guv?'

'Go and have another word with Olga Brewster. Ask her if she had any problems with Brendan or if he had mentioned moving to another B&B.'

'Okay, guv.' She started to move away, then turned back to Callum. 'Wouldn't she have told Bird when he went to see her?'

'Possibly, but generally speaking, people are more likely to mention success than they are failure. There could have been something she was not completely happy about with her guest that made her ask him to leave, but she didn't want to mention it. And Bird thought she was holding something back when he spoke to her. She might open up to you.'

Callum watched as Legs lifted her furry-collared coat from the rack behind the door and went out into the corridor. He returned to his chair. It could be that Brendan had not told Olga he was intending to move on because he didn't want to upset his host. Callum pulled his sketch towards him. But sparing people's feelings and Brendan Stafford did not sit easily in the same sentence.

A message pinged up on his screen. Brendan Stafford's tox report was clear. No drugs and no alcohol in his system when he died. That ruled out him being easily overcome in the fight because he was incapacitated by drugs or alcohol. But Martha had said there was little evidence that he had attempted to fight back. She was still trying to match the profile of the murder weapon. There were no defence wounds on his arms, and no evidence from his hands that he had attempted to retaliate. Callum added a decorative ridge to the roof of a thatched cottage in his drawing. Perhaps Brendan had raised his hands to protect his face but his assailant, or assailants, had been concentrating on disabling, rather than disfiguring, the man.

Perhaps the reason Crossways Farm was entered into Brendan's satnav was because either Keiron or Penny was his missing relative. Abigail had told them that both the thatcher and the hurdle maker rented barns down the track than ran behind the stables at the lower end of the Garlands' property. Perhaps, when Charlie and her little sister had seen Brendan standing in their yard, it was because he had been down to the barns and was on his way back up to the village and not because he was returning from a walk on the forest as the girls had thought.

Callum called to Cookie, who came into the fishbowl.

'I want you to check into any possible connection between Brendan, Keiron Tapper and Penny Hopwood,' Callum said. 'We need to establish if either of them has a prior connection to Brendan, and that includes the possibility that one of them could be a member of the mysterious local family that was the supposed reason Brendan was moving here.'

'Okey-cokey, guv. And the door-to-door for the Friday that he died hasn't turned up anything yet. Lots of people were at the meeting but none of them saw anything suspicious on their way to the village hall. We had a word with the people that were in the pub, as far as the staff could help us with names, but nothing there.' Cookie bobbed from one foot to the other, and then back again. 'There's two from the door-to-door that I'm following up on for a bit more clarification. But nothing in his movements for that Friday, so far, is flagging up any sort of confrontation between him and anyone. He had lunch in the Drunken Donkey, and he went in the shop later that afternoon. But that's it.'

'Let me know what you find,' Callum said to the back of Cookie's head as the junior officer scuttled back to his desk and turned his attention to his computer.

Chapter Sixteen

Daisy caught Callum's eye as he walked in through the outer office, and he paused when he reached her desk.

'Legs was telling me something this morning about Lucy Cozens and Eddie Gilligan. Did she mention it to you?'

Callum shook his head.

'Oh, I thought she might. Actually, I'm not sure it's really relevant but it could be worth noting, perhaps.'

Callum nodded his head towards the fishbowl and heard Daisy push back her chair and follow him. He sat and she hitched a hip on the edge of his desk.

'Legs said that Gloria told her that Lucy was having a relationship with someone local behind Eddie's back,' Daisy said.

'We already know that,' Callum said. If Legs hadn't mentioned any new information before he sent her off to see Olga Brewster, it was probably because it was nothing more than unsubstantiated gossip. 'And?'

'And about a fortnight ago, Gloria went to a baby shower. Legs was supposed to go but she was still working and missed it.'

'And?'

'Lucy was there. Near the end of the get-together, when they had got through a couple of bottles of prosecco, Lucy got a phone call. She was a bit tipsy, pink-cheeked and giggly. Gloria was sitting next to her on the sofa, and she is sure it was a man's voice at the other end. Lucy ended the call by whispering, "I'll be five minutes. Go and warm up the bed." The house they were at was just down the road from the Drunken Donkey, on Woodgreen Road, so it must be someone in the village.'

'That is logical, but I can't see how that's relevant. A fortnight ago, Brendan was still in Birmingham. Let's concentrate on his murder for now, please,' Callum said. Nevertheless, he did a quick calculation and concluded that it would take more than five minutes to walk from the Drunken Donkey to Eddie's out-of-the-way cottage.

'Legs probably didn't think it was relevant,' said Daisy, 'but it made me wonder who the man was, being as how we now know he lives in the middle of the village.'

Daisy stood away from his desk. 'And the other thing Legs said, which is very totally not relevant to us, is that Legs thinks that Gloria is getting broody.' Daisy grinned at him and went into the outer office.

That was all he needed, officers cooing over babies when they should be concentrating on the job.

Callum went to the back wall of the outer office and studied the map pinned up there. He heard footsteps behind him and smelled Daisy's apple shampoo as she joined him.

'I was just thinking,' she said. 'You remember Eddie's best mate, Sebastian something, who went to see him the morning after Eddie got drunk?'

'Sebastian Wells,' Callum supplied.

'That's right, Wells.' She pressed her finger to the map. 'Well, he lives here, halfway between Eddie's and the Drunken Donkey. You don't suppose he could be the away-day lover?'

'I don't suppose anything,' Callum said and went into the fishbowl to answer his ringing phone.

'MacLean,' he said, having stretched his arm across his desk to lift the receiver.

'Jimmy, here.' His breath came in short puffs.

Callum could hear other voices calling and the blares of cattle in close proximity to the agister and wondered what was happening.

'Now shut the gate,' Jimmy shouted across to someone. 'Sorry about that, Cal. Some steers escaped and I've been giving them a hand to round them up. We've just got them back in the field.' He exhaled a long breath. 'Running's harder than it used to be. Right, I liaised with Forestry England and the keeper asked me to find out what I could. I said I'd have a look for the spent cartridge up in Pitts Wood Inclosure, and I found it. It's a ballistic-tipped Nosler, home-packed. They're pretty common and lots of stalkers pack their own rather than buying from a gunsmith.'

There was a snick as Jimmy opened the door of his pickup and said, 'Move over.'

Callum heard the whine of his collie, Panda, and the caws of the rooks and blares of the cattle were muted by his door closing.

'It was about a hundred and fifty metre shot, so a pretty good distance.' Jimmy started his engine. 'I've got to go and see a man about a dog but if I learn anything else I'll let you know.'

'Wait,' Callum said. 'What was the gun?'

'Sorry, thought I'd said. It was a triple two, a .222 to you, mate.' Jimmy cancelled the connection.

Callum looked up as Bird appeared in the doorway to the fishbowl.

'The Salisbury firm of solicitors, Waterman and White, that Brendan engaged to deal with the conveyancing, just phoned me back, guv,' Bird said. 'He had no previous connection to them, so they have no knowledge of either his divorce or his will. Brendan just used them because he was buying a property in the area, and he thought it would be easier. He told them it made more sense to engage a local crew who knew the ropes and who they were dealing with so it should speed up the process.'

'As we thought,' Callum said.

'Yes, the chap said Brendan seemed keen to get the ball rolling, even though he hadn't actually made an offer on any house as yet, so he was pretty keen about moving down here. Then I had a word with the Birmingham solicitor who acted for him when he got divorced. He said he wished they were all that easy. He gave me the details.' Bird sent a questioning look to Callum.

'Yes, go on,' Callum said.

'It just confirms what Victoria told us. They split the proceeds of the jointly owned property half-half. He kept his car, and she kept hers – I think he did better in that deal – and they each kept their own pension entitlements, so she got the better deal there, I reckon,' Bird said.

'That does sound unusual,' Callum said, 'a non-acrimonious divorce.'

'Certainly does. Probably less complicated as they haven't got any kids,' Bird said, leaning his shoulder against the door jamb.

'Did you ask about his will?' Callum said.

'Yeah.' Bird stood away from the door frame, weight on both feet, poised to move. 'The bloke I spoke to is sure that Brendan did make a new will but not with him. They're quite a big concern and he used a colleague in the firm who specialises in that sort of thing. They're going to get someone to dig it out and then give me a ring back.' He returned to his desk.

Chapter Seventeen

'Bird.' Callum walked out of the fishbowl and paused beside the constable, who was seated at his desk. 'See who has a licence for a .222 locally.' He pushed his arms into the sleeves of his jacket. 'And check up on who holds a game licence while you're at it.' Just because nobody had told Jimmy Eastwood or the keeper that they were out shooting deer, it did not necessarily make the cull illegal. Callum wasn't keen on the possibility of an unlicensed gun holder running around on his patch.

'Wilco, guv.' Bird made a note on his pad of paper then looked up at Callum. 'Urgent?' he asked.

'Not especially,' Callum said. 'Daisy and I are off to see Penny and Keiron at Crossways Farm. Put it on my desk, please.'

Callum went out into the corridor and heard the door of the office close behind Daisy as she caught up with him, zipping her jacket closed as she walked.

'Do you reckon they'll give us an allowance for thermal underwear if this cold snap continues?' She skipped a step to keep up with him.

Callum glanced down at her, ignored her question, then held open the door for her to proceed him out into the car park.

'I had to break the ice on Moses's water trough this morning.' She zapped open her Navara. 'I hope this weather shoots off to somewhere that it'll be appreciated, like a ski resort.'

'I'll see what I can arrange,' Callum said closing the passenger door. 'Now drive.'

She grinned across the cab at him and pulled smoothly away from the station car park.

* * *

When Daisy indicated to turn onto the gravel track to Crossways Farm, she had to wait as a herd of donkeys ambled across the track in front of her. They walked slowly with short, stilted strides, their small hooves making no indents in the frosted ground.

'Now that's what you call a winter coat,' Daisy said, pointing at the last donkey in the queue, who had a thick covering of shaggy brown hair.

When the last beast had crossed in front of her, she drove over the cattle grid onto the track, and Callum saw in his peripheral vision the donkey herd gather outside the picket fence of the Drunken Donkey pub.

They drove past the house and stables. Abigail's Defender and the little Fiat were parked in the cobbled yard, but Callum saw no signs of life. They followed the track down towards the barns where birds circled above the buildings in a vortex, like black rags whirling in the breeze. Grey clouds formed a backdrop, gathering and hovering low in the sky. They looked heavy and had a pinkness about them that made Callum think of snow.

Daisy stopped outside the barns. 'There's nobody here,' she said, switching off her engine. 'That's where they usually park.' She pointed to an area in front of each barn where the gravel had visible tyre indentations, the crests of which were frosted into ridges like cake icing.

It was obvious which tenant used which barn. The right hand of the pair was evidently Penny's domain. The double galvanised doors were padlocked closed, and a pile of completed hurdles was stacked neatly to the side of the doorway. The remainder of the outside space was clear of clutter. By contrast, the other barn doors were open, one trigged back behind a block of wood, the other swinging free. Straw from breached sheaves had been disturbed by the wind, or perhaps animals, and was scattered along the side of the building. A couple of gorilla tubs visible amidst the debris had tools in them, and a ladder that had once been vertical against the barn had slid sideways prescribing an arc of dents in the galvanised wall before coming to rest on top of the discarded straw.

'Guess which one is rented by Keiron,' Daisy said before opening her door and getting out of the Navara.

Callum watched through the windscreen as Daisy walked to the building and peered inside. She looked back at Callum, shook her head and shrugged before coming back to her vehicle.

'No one in sight,' she said, closing the door behind her, diminishing the noisy caws of the rooks. 'I have no idea how he finds anything in that barn. It could do with a good clear-up. There's a tallet at the far end…'

'A what?' Callum interrupted.

'Tallet, a sort of wooden loft you store hay on. Except he seems to have a bed on it so perhaps he sleeps here sometimes. The place is absolutely filthy, dirty cups and stuff everywhere.'

Callum thought it fortunate that she had not yet seen the inside of Hope Cottage with his stacks of partially unpacked boxes.

'Perhaps he sleeps up there when he has one too many at the Donkey; it's just across the road,' she continued. 'No point in us waiting, is there? Where to now, Callum?' She turned her vehicle around and Callum could feel their tyres jolting over the frozen ruts in the gravel surface.

'Station,' Callum said when she had completed the manoeuvre.

When the track widened as they neared Crossways Farmhouse, the camper van with its bed and breakfast guests was pulling to a stop in front of the house, the brake lights shining through the gloom of the greying afternoon.

'The Palmer brothers must have just got back,' Daisy said. 'They weren't there when we came in.'

The passenger door of the camper van opened, and a man clothed in a heavy tweed jacket dropped down onto the cobbles. The binoculars hanging from a neck strap bounced upwards when he landed heavily on both feet. He stumbled and reached out a hand towards the rear side door of the vehicle. He looked as if he was going to open it but stopped when he saw their vehicle and instead slapped his hand on the bodywork to steady himself. He turned his head and said something to the driver, who was still inside the vehicle.

'That's the man who was in the passenger seat the first time we came here,' Daisy said. 'The one who stuck his head out when I stopped beside him.'

'Must be the other brother. He looks as if he's had one or two,' Callum said.

The driver, who had now disembarked, walked around the rear of their vehicle to stand beside his brother. He raised a hand to the detectives and Callum acknowledged the greeting. The men stood together, watching as Daisy drove on along the track and headed for the road.

'They must need their heads read going out in this temperature to look for birds.' Daisy shivered theatrically.

'They were dressed for the weather,' Callum said. 'But each to their own.'

Daisy's tyres rumbled over the cattle grid, and she paused before pulling out onto the road. The donkeys were still congregated outside the fence of the pub, reminding Callum of the loitering gangs of youths in Glasgow on a Friday evening.

* * *

'On your desk, guv.' Bird tipped his head towards the fishbowl when Callum and Daisy returned to the office.

'Thanks, Bird.' Callum felt the warmth in his office compared with the outside temperature and hung his jacket on the clothes stand in the corner. He wondered how good it was for the body to be breathing in the crisp chilled air of outdoors, then entering the fuggy dust-laden atmosphere of the office. He put his phone on his desk. Perhaps Rain would ring and then he could ask her for her opinion.

He looked at the two sheets of paper that Bird had put on his desk and compared the information. One name jumped out at him – Sebastian Wells. When Miles was looking after Eddie following his lapse, Sebastian was the friend who had visited him at his cottage. The man held a licence for a Parker Hale .222. He was also a member of the National Gamekeepers' Organisation and was certified to shoot game and sell it.

He looked across the office and saw that Bird was already looking in his direction. He beckoned to him with a nod of his head.

'Bird,' Callum said, as the officer came to the doorway and leaned against the jamb. 'Give Sebastian Wells a call and ask him if he shot the deer in Pitts Wood, please.' That should help clear up the question of poachers for Jimmy Eastwood. It could just be a legal cull, and word had not got back to the agister or keeper.

'I'll give him a bell,' Bird said. 'Four of five days ago, wasn't it?'

Callum nodded. 'And ask him where he sells the game he shoots.'

'There's a game shop just outside Downton on the trading estate that supplies restaurants, and I know they have stalls at farmers' markets. Helen buys stuff from them sometimes at Salisbury market. And there's always Harry Kingman, the butcher in Fordingbridge.'

‘Check it out. Anything back from the solicitors about Brendan’s beneficiaries?’

Bird shook his head. ‘Not yet, guv.’

‘Chase it, Bird.’ If Brendan has traced this unknown relative and shared with them that they would benefit in the event of his death, it gave them a motive for murder.

Cookie jumped up from his chair and came across to Callum’s office as Bird walked back to his desk.

‘Guv, there’s been another burglary. Earlier on today, and in broad daylight.’ Cookie shook the piece of paper he held, as if it might sprinkle the details of the misdemeanour at his feet.

‘Where?’ Callum asked. He hoped it wasn’t another golfing pal of Bellman’s.

‘Woodgreen. Just up from the village green.’

‘What was taken this time? Is it the same people?’ Callum asked. This was the first one that had occurred in daylight.

‘Cash, I think, guv. It was on the kitchen table and that is all that’s missing. The Pearsons went out and when they got back the postman had put some letters on the kitchen table and the money was gone.’

‘Check what the neighbours saw. Let me know what you find – as soon as you can.’

He expected that, as soon as Bellman heard about this latest theft, he would be summoned for an update. Bellman had a bee in his bonnet about the burglaries now that a friend of his had been targeted.

Callum wanted to hurry the investigation along and get some answers so that he could concentrate on the murder of Brendan Stafford. The only evidence of speed in this investigation was Cookie. The lad’s energy levels never seemed to drop, and he seldom sat still.

Callum returned to his seat. If he had still been in Glasgow his initial response would have been to make the postman his number one suspect. That man had a knowledge of the people and properties on his round and was, to some extent, invisible. But during the last three years, Callum had realised that in this rural setting a postman played a very different role from that of his counterpart in the city. Here they fulfilled a variety of tasks from trusted friend to stock drover when a helping hand was needed. They would sign for packages and put them in a safe place if the recipient was not at home, check on the elderly and collect letters to save people a trip to the post box. He was also aware that this particular delivery route had been worked by the same man for over twenty years, which in itself indicated trustworthiness. He checked his computer and found that not only did the postman have no criminal record, but he also had a clean driving licence, which must constitute some sort of miracle for a man who spent his working life behind the wheel.

Chapter Eighteen

In mid-afternoon the temperature began to drop, and Callum knew that they were in for another freezing night. He had just decided to go back to Crossways Farm to see if Keiron and Penny were back when Cookie scooted into the doorway of the fishbowl.

'I've got the stuff you wanted about the latest burglary, guv.'

Callum beckoned him in. If Cookie remained standing, his constant movement made Callum feel seasick. He pointed to the chair on the visitor's side of the desk and Cookie perched on the edge of the seat but looked ready to spring into action at a second's notice.

'What do we know? Facts, please, Cookie, not speculation.' Callum picked up his pen to make notes.

'The people are called the Pearsons – Mum and Dad and a grown-up son – and they are smallholders with forest rights so that most of their stock runs loose on the Forest.'

That was not an unusual state of affairs. Many commoners who had the right to graze cattle and ponies on the open heaths for an annual fee, owned little land of their own and just maintained a few buildings for winter housing or fodder storage.

'They've got a few sheep that they keep down in a field in Woodgreen and they are due to lamb.' Cookie looked up at Callum, perhaps to check that he was giving the information required.

'Go on,' Callum said.

Cookie settled back in the chair. 'Well, somebody phoned them to say that one of the sheep had just got out so they all three dashed out to find her before she disappeared. They took the dog with them in the back of the pickup. Apparently, they knew which ewe it would be – actually they pronounced it *yow* – because she did the same thing last year, too. As soon as she is going to lamb, she escapes or tries to.'

Callum knew from Daisy that the wild New Forest ponies, when they were due to foal, often isolated themselves from the rest of the herd. 'Did they find the sheep?' Callum asked.

'Yes. She was just up the track. No harm done. They didn't lock their door when they went out because they left in a hurry. Earlier that morning, Mrs Pearson had sold a couple of bales of hay to a horsey woman who paid cash when she collected them. It wasn't much money, and she left it on the kitchen table. When they got back it was gone, and the letters were in its place.'

Callum was getting used to the fact that many people, when they left their houses for a short time, didn't lock their doors. It was something he had never come across in Glasgow.

'Did they see anyone about when they left?'

'Mrs Pearson said they passed the postman a few houses down from theirs, and that makes sense because the letters were on the table when they got back. They passed a couple of cars and some damn-fool tourist in a motorhome tootling up the middle of the road, slowing them down. Her son said she's got a thing about tourists; she thinks they leave gates open and drop litter everywhere.'

Callum thought that Mrs Pearson might be right. He knew that they often failed to understand the importance of leaving gates the way that you found them. If a gate was closed it was closed for a good reason.

'Have a word with the postman for the record. I don't consider him a suspect, but he might have seen something helpful,' Callum said.

'Onto it, guv.' Cookie rose to his feet and sped out of the fishbowl in one fluid movement.

* * *

Bellman's office had seemed a deeper shade of grey than usual, and Callum was pleased to close the door behind him and head back to his own office. As he had surmised, the latest burglary was playing on Bellman's mind. Callum had pre-empted any summons that his superior might have been going to issue by going and tapping on his door. Bellman had again mentioned the prestigious timepiece that had been won in a high-profile golf tournament. It had taken pride of place amongst the larger trophies on display in the man's sitting room. The now empty space annoyed the golfer and he, in turn, passed his annoyance onto Bellman who shared it with Callum.

Callum had listened quietly to his superior officer until he had been dismissed. It was only when he reached out to open the door to their own office that he realised Bellman had not asked for an update on the investigation into the murder of Brendan Stafford.

* * *

Daisy drove slowly along Roger Penny Way past the Drunken Donkey pub. Callum looked across to the vehicles parked on the gravel outside. It seemed unexpectedly busy for a freezing Tuesday afternoon in mid-winter. A blue-and-cream Dormobile was parked closest to the building and Callum wondered if there were others, besides the Palmer brothers, who were birdwatching in the area. Whatever that vehicle was doing in the New Forest, the occupants would need to be very hardy to sleep in it at night in this weather.

'I reckon Penny and Keiron will be back by now. It must be too cold to work outside in this temperature, don't you think?' Daisy said.

'That's what we're doing,' he said.

'You know what I mean. Why didn't you just ring them and ask them if they knew Brendan Stafford?' She stopped swiftly as two ponies walked off the left-side verge and ambled across the tarmac in front of her. Animals had the right of way in the National Park and drivers were expected to keep their welfare in mind as they journeyed along the forest roads.

'I want to see their reactions when I ask them. I can't do that on the phone.' Callum followed the progress of the ponies towards the pub side of the road.

Chapter Nineteen

Daisy was sliding the car into gear to pull away, when Callum noticed the pub door opening. A young man in jeans and a green tweed jacket came out. He paused to look up at the sky, then took a cap from his pocket and put it on.

'That's Sebastian Wells, isn't it?' Callum said.

Daisy looked across. 'One and the same,' she said and looked at Callum.

Callum pointed his finger towards the pub. Daisy drove onto the gravel surround and parked next to the Dormobile. When Seb made to walk behind their Navara en route to his vehicle, Callum opened his passenger door and introduced himself.

'Can you spare us a couple of minutes?' Callum asked.

Seb nodded.

Callum reached his arm behind his seat into the back of the crew cab and opened the rear door. 'Hop in. I won't keep you long, but it'll be warmer inside.'

Seb got into the car and nodded a greeting to Daisy, who had swivelled round in her seat.

'What's this about?' he asked.

He was fair-skinned, cheeks pink with the cold, his brow furrowed. He rubbed the back of his hand across his mouth. His fingers were chapped and rough with dirt-lines beneath his nails.

'Just routine. Nothing to worry about,' Callum said.

'Ask away.' Seb pushed back the cuff of his left sleeve. 'I've got another job to get to. I just stopped into the Donkey because they asked me to quote for levelling out a bit of the pub garden before Easter. I've got a JCB. Sideline.'

That answered the unasked question about why he was in the pub in the middle of the working day. 'It was about your rifle, your .222,' Callum said.

The tension eased from Seb's shoulders. 'It's at home, in a gun cabinet. It's locked and in the back house where my dogs are. Safe as houses. Why?'

'I've seen your dogs,' Daisy said. 'That sounds like a pretty safe place to me.'

Callum looked questioningly at Daisy. He had no idea what Seb meant by a back house.

'The dogs are kept in a room of their own at the back of the house. It would be a brave man who tried to steal a gun with them in the room.' Daisy grinned at Seb.

Seb's face softened. 'Don't tell, but they're a pushover with people they know. They play with our nipper as gentle as anything.'

Callum thought that large dogs and small children were not a good combination, but what did he know? He was not responsible for either.

'Do you lend your gun to anyone?' Callum asked.

'Nope. That's what the other policeman asked me when he phoned me a couple of minutes ago. I told him that I haven't shot any deer recently, and if I had, I would have told the keeper. I've never let anyone borrow my gun either. Can I go now?' Seb reached for the door handle, tension tightening his movements.

Callum wondered if it was possible that anyone, particularly a friend, could have helped himself to the weapon and returned it without Seb knowing about it.

Seb's assurance that his dogs were very friendly to people they knew was not very reassuring.

'Yes. That's all I wanted to ask you.' Callum turned towards the front of the vehicle.

'How's Eddie Gilligan coming along now?' Daisy asked. 'Miles told us you went to see him.'

Callum gave her a hard look, a frown ridging his brow, but she avoided his eye contact.

Seb's features relaxed into a smile, and he let go of the door handle. 'He's doing good. He's best rid of Lucy.'

'Why?' Daisy asked with an encouraging smile.

'Because she's a money-grabbing little cow. She was just using him for what she could get out of him.'

'Didn't Eddie realise that?' Daisy asked.

'Nope. He was smitten, hook line and sinker. We thought he'd work it out when she kept asking for more and more. Did he hell. He bought her an engagement ring instead. That was a waste of money.' Seb gave a shake of his head.

'Did you, or his other friends share your concerns with him?' Callum asked.

'Would you?' Seb countered. 'Nope. We didn't have the heart because he was the happiest we'd seen him since his dad… uh… died. Well, to begin with anyway. We just hoped he'd see through her.'

Callum nodded. 'So, what happened?'

'She was two-timing him, wasn't she. He was my best mate, best man at our wedding, so I told Eddie. He confronted her in the Donkey, and she laughed in his face and threw the ring back at him. You should have heard her. She hasn't half got a tongue on her.'

Callum acknowledged the subtle differences with the other retelling of the encounter. Lucy had told her friends that she was keeping the ring and had every right to keep it. He was inclined to believe that Lucy had given Eddie back his ring and was painting herself as a victim.

'Who was she seeing?' Daisy asked. 'Not you?'

Seb gave her a hard look. 'Do me a favour.' He sounded disgusted at the thought. 'No one in their right mind would touch her with a bargepole, not now, and not then because she was Eddie's.'

The windows had misted up and Daisy swept her sleeve across the inside of her windscreen. The smell of wet dog was leaching from Seb's jacket with the warmth.

'Telling Eddie must have been difficult,' Callum said. 'Are you still friends?'

'Yeah. He took it out on me at first, shoot the messenger and all that, but I've been to see him a couple of times and he has forgiven me. I reckon, if he hadn't ended it, she would have finished him off.'

Callum nodded. Seb opened the door, got out and stood beside the car.

'How did you know she was seeing someone else?' Callum asked.

Seb dipped his head back into the cab. 'She was in the pub one night, had a phone call, left and when she came back, she was all flushed cheeks and bright eyes.' He looked directly at Callum. 'There's nothing wrong with my sense of smell.'

'Thanks for your time,' Callum said as the door snicked closed.

Seb walked around the rear of their Navara to a grey pickup with a battered canopy cover over the cargo bed.

Callum rubbed his arm across the misted passenger window as Seb pulled out of the car park and carefully negotiated the two ponies who had moved from the verge to stand in the middle of the road.

Daisy reversed clear of the Dormobile and stopped before joining the road. Her front tyres dropped into two well-worn ruts that were filled with ice-edged water. He was about to ask her why the ponies chose to stand in the middle of the road when she made a disappointed noise.

'Problem?' he asked.

'There,' she nodded her head towards the track that led down to Crossways Farm. Both Keiron and Penny drove out onto Roger Penny Way, one behind the other, and headed off in different directions.

'Tomorrow will have to do,' Callum said. 'Let's get back to the station.'

Chapter Twenty

'Guv?' Legs called across the room as Callum held the office door open for Daisy to enter in front of him.

As he crossed the office, the overhead lights threw distorted shadows across the floor. These morphed together and pooled at his feet when he stood by her desk.

'How did you get on with Olga Brewster?' he asked.

'All right, but she still seems a bit shocked by what's happened. She had some repairs done to her thatched ridge last week and when I got there, she was walking round the garden clutching a framed photo of her daughter, Nadia. She was picking up bits of straw with her left hand from around a sort of shrine she has set up to her. She didn't even have a coat on. When I took the photo off her and suggested we go inside, her hands were freezing.'

'What did she say about Brendan?' Daisy said, coming to join them.

'That he was more than happy at hers and had just told her he was going to stay for at least another week and probably longer. That was fine by her, particularly as he paid in advance.'

January was the kipper season for tourism, so Brendan had plenty of other bed and breakfasts he could have moved to if he didn't like his current accommodation. If he had paid in advance he was clearly not intending to move on, so why had he plumbed Crossways Farm into his satnav?

'Did Brendan mention Crossways Farm to Olga?'

Legs shook her head. 'But he did tell her he was a retired lecturer, which we know is true and that he was going to do a course in photography. Olga has framed photos all round her sitting room. When she told me where the one she had taken outside lived and I put it back for her, she said it was of her daughter who had died.'

'That's sad,' Daisy said. 'People expect their kids to live longer than them.'

'Doubly sad in this case,' Legs said. 'Some of the other photos were of her husband who was killed in a car crash about seven years ago, and that's the reason she moved down south.'

'Poor Olga,' Daisy said.

'She's a bit fragile and seems quite distracted. She said that Brendan admired her photos and went round the room picking them all up and looking at them. That's when he told her he had family connections down here. But despite her asking, he didn't mention any names.'

'Thanks, Legs,' Callum said, unfastening his coat. 'Anything else?'

'When he left hers on Friday morning, he asked her where the local graveyard was. She was going to ask him about it when he came back that evening, but, as we know, he never made it back. Perhaps he was doing his family tree and wanted to look at the headstones, or he might have been looking to reserve a plot for himself if he has family here.'

'Both are points to consider. And where is the graveyard?' Callum asked. He could not remember seeing one in the village.

'It's the one out on the Stuckton Road.'

'Did you find out anything else?' Callum asked.

'Not really,' Legs said. 'She just complained about how untidy Keiron was, and said, if I didn't have any more questions she was going to Crossways Farm to get some eggs and give her dogs a walk.'

'Is her cottage really decorated with pink roses everywhere, like Bird said?' Daisy asked.

Legs nodded. 'Pretty much.'

Daisy looked up at Callum. 'Don't you think that's an odd choice of décor for a man? With so many empty B&Bs at this time of the year, he could have stayed anywhere. Why did he choose that one?'

'Whatever his reason for choosing it, he was obviously happy with his choice if he paid to stay longer,' Callum said and went into the fishbowl.

He had never felt any compunction to trace his own family tree. Both his parents had several siblings who had all married and he had a whole raft of cousins, most of whom he had met at regular family gatherings before he had come south. He missed them all, his three sisters especially, but they kept in touch over the airwaves. He felt a sort of reassurance in knowing where he came from, that he would follow the physical path of his father and his grandfather, morph into them as time passed. As a child he had loved to hear stories of earlier generations. It was an anchor for him.

Who had Brendan been looking for? It would have been helpful if Cookie had found details of a great Auntie Flo, or a Grandpa Soames in his online contacts, but he hadn't. Callum looked into the outer office and saw Cookie take something out of a drawer, unwrap it and take a large bite. A chocolate bar of some kind. No wonder he had boundless energy. Callum went to stand beside the lad.

'Cookie,' Callum said. 'Did you find anything on Brendan's laptop to suggest he was tracing his family tree? A membership to Ancestry or similar?'

Cookie swallowed quickly. 'No, guv.' He frowned before continuing. 'Do you think he was looking for dead relatives then, not live ones?'

'It's possible. Check with his solicitor and bank. See if he has come into some money, a legacy,' Callum said.

Callum went back to the fishbowl and sank onto his chair to think. He sketched a headstone on the edge of a sheet of paper. It had been a consideration, if a very slim one, that Brendan had searched for, and found, a local relative and that they had killed him. Cookie had not been able to find a single reference to a family connection in the New Forest, let alone the village. If Brendan was chasing the past, it closed off one line of investigation, because the dead could not kill. Callum felt as if he was driving around a giant roundabout and despite the exit signs was unable to see the road he needed to take.

Bird had still not managed to pin down the errant will-maker but had been promised a phone call first thing in the morning. Brendan's ex-wife was out of the country when Brendan was murdered and was adamant that she would not benefit from his death. If he believed Victoria, which he did, Brendan had not kept in close contact with his only cousin. Cookie had checked all the door-to-door statements and there were no reported sightings of Brendan, either alone, or in the company of other persons on the evening he was killed. There were no threatening emails or messages from any of his past conquests, or their parents or lawyers, not even the dean. So, who had wanted Brendan dead? Who should they be looking for?

'Bird,' Callum called to him. 'See what you can find about Brendan and his past relationships, please.' Just because nobody had sent him a threatening letter did not mean that nobody wished him harm.

* * *

Callum picked up an envelope from the mat, his eye drawn by a trail of small pieces of white paper that prescribed a path to the cat tree. He walked towards it, collecting the shreds of paper as he went. He had never seen Amber do anything other than ignore the cat tree, so he was surprised to see her curled into the hammock. An envelope was partially visible, the remainder of it concealed beneath her body, and a confetti of torn paper fragments littered the wooden floor beneath the climber. He stretched out a hand to fuss the cat, then eased his letter from beneath her purring body. One end of the envelope had survived unscathed, but the other had chunks torn out of it, and the adjacent paper was perforated with teeth marks.

'You're a wee beastie, aren't you? Were you fed up? Look what you've done to my post.' Callum used his thumb to slit open the envelope and extracted a sheet of paper, the top left corner of which was missing. 'Bank statement, so no bother.' He picked up the pieces of paper from the floor around the cat tree, put them in the envelope and stroked the feline. 'I promise to let you out very soon; Daisy says three more weeks.' He went into the kitchen.

Amber climbed out of the hammock, crossed one of the platforms and jumped down onto the floor. She stood beside Callum and miaowed as he prepared her food. He knew she was bored with captivity and frustrated that she couldn't get out, but at least she was very good about using the litter tray and he was grateful for that.

The house was near silent as he prepared his supper, the few sounds being the scrape of the cat bowl across the floor and the bubbling of the water in the kettle. He missed Rain humming or singing as she cooked. She would catch his eye and smile at him and that made his heart flutter like an emerging butterfly. He switched the television on to an audio station and lowered the volume.

Later that evening he unpacked a couple more boxes and flattened them for recycling. He wondered if there was a record of the longest time it had taken a person to unpack after moving house. With a glass of whisky in hand, he took his sketch pad down to the sofa and changed stations to the television news. He caught the tail end of a sports report about Ronnie O'Sullivan being both the oldest and youngest player to win the snooker Masters tournament, and then a less-than-impressive weather forecast of snow for the entire country. Not a single flake had dropped from the sky since he moved south, and he almost longed to see white flakes fluttering earthward. He remembered his grandfather coming down from the hill, his thick tweed jacket hanging with miniature icicles. When Callum had commented on the bad weather, he had been told there was no such thing as bad weather, just the wrong clothes.

Amber landed soundlessly on the cushion beside him and curled up, leaning against his thigh. The warmth of her body seeped through his jeans, and he could feel the vibration of her purr.

'You're lucky to have to stay indoors, wee beastie, with weather like that on the way.'

Chapter Twenty-One

Callum drove along Roger Penny Way, heading towards Fordingbridge and work. The low sun strobed in his eyes, but clouds were beginning to gather in the sky, crowding behind one another, being pulled down towards the land by their heavy grey bases. The wind was rising, and he felt it was going to rain today and not snow as the meteorologists had suggested.

A battered pickup travelling in front of him suddenly slowed to a crawl. The open bed had a couple of small bales of hay on it and these jostled against each other as the nearside tyres of the vehicle rolled up onto the verge. The pickup blasted its horn four times and stopped moving. Callum slowed and lowered his passenger window, preparing to pass and ask the driver if he had a problem. As he drew level, the driver shouted 'come on' through his open passenger window. He was answered by a shrill whinny from across the heather and a herd of ponies erupted from a stand of gorse bushes and trotted single file behind the vehicle as it turned off the road onto a parking area. Breakfast on the hoof, Callum thought as he saw the driver exit his vehicle. Accelerating away, Callum looked in his rearview mirror and saw the man throw pats of hay to his stock.

The herd of donkeys had moved from outside the pub and had threaded themselves between the grey trunks of a stand of gorse on the opposite side of the road. Approaching the village hall, Callum recognised the familiar figure of Susie Treadwell leaving the phone box library, closing the door behind her and going into the bus shelter, a book in her hand. He checked the time on his dashboard and thought that at this hour of the morning she should have been on her way to school. With her lust for learning, he thought it was unlikely that she would be playing truant, so there was probably another legitimate reason for her absence.

When his tyres crunched to a stop on the gravel, Callum could see Susie through the doorless opening. She looked up and gave him a little wave.

He lowered his window and rested his arm along the sill. 'No school?' he asked, his voice carrying clearly across the verge.

Susie shook her head. As before, she sat sideways on the bench seat, and having lifted her feet up onto it, she was leaning her back against the side wall. 'Inset day. I just finished *A Room with a View*, so I came to change my book. Have you ever been to Italy?'

He and Grace had honeymooned in Florence. 'I have. It is very beautiful.'

'I'm going to go there myself, one day.' She looked beyond Callum at the sound of screeching brakes and the skid of tyres on the tarmac road. Callum turned round in time to see Keiron judder to a stop and blow his horn at a pony, who was ambling across the verges and driveways, obstructing the entrance to Crossways Farm. The animal ignored him and Keiron revved his engine until his way was clear, and he could turn off the road.

'He's always so angry,' Susie said and shook her head.

'Always?' Callum said. 'Have you seen him angry before?'

Susie pulled her knees up towards her chest and looped her arms around them, the book in her lap. She was still wearing the too-large raincoat with the sleeves folded back. 'Last week, I was in here reading and he came out of the Donkey' – she nodded her head towards the pub on the other side of the road – 'and a man was just getting back in his car when Keiron came out and started shouting at him and waving his arms about.'

'Who was the other man?' Callum asked.

'I don't know him, but he was tall with skinny black jeans and bleached hair.'

It sounded very much like Brendan Stafford from her description.

'Can you recall what his car was like?'

'Of course,' Susie said. 'It was bright blue, a bit in your face actually, and it was the make with the Olympic rings on the front.'

'That's very observant of you.'

'Getting angry doesn't get him anywhere. It just makes other people angry, too,' Susie said.

'It does that,' Callum said. 'What happened next?'

Susie brushed her fringe back from her eyes. 'Keiron stabbed his finger at the man's chest, but the man just laughed and got in his car and drove away. Keiron shouted after him and shook his fist. He was so angry that he kicked his own tyre. Then he got in his pickup, slammed the door and drove off. His music was too loud.' She looked at Callum with a confident gaze. 'Do you know a lady writer called Maya Angelou?' She waited for him to nod and then continued, 'I think she said something about every storm eventually running out of rain, or something like that, I can't quite remember. Do you think Keiron will ever stop being angry?'

Callum met her earnest eyes. He could not remember how he had viewed the world when he was thirteen and neither could he un-know what he knew now. He was unsure what sort of answer she expected from him, but he was conscious that he didn't want to disappoint her.

'Some folks are their own worst enemy and make their own world difficult to live in.' After a moment he added, 'I think it's good to concentrate on what makes the world work for you, what makes your world a nice place to live.'

'Moral compass, you mean.' She laughed aloud. 'You'll catch flies,' she said.

Callum realised she was referring to his mouth having opened in surprise at her remark. He closed it and grinned at her. 'If you like,' he said, and removing his arm from the sill, hovered his hand over the window controls. This child was thirteen going on thirty.

'Mum says I read too much but Uncle Vinny says we could all do to read a bit more.' She straightened her legs along the bench and opened the book across her thighs. 'See you later, alligator.'

'In a while, crocodile,' he answered before he could stop himself. He smiled as he pulled away from the verge, raising his window as he drove back onto the tarmac. How much would it take for angry Keiron to progress from stabbing with his finger to stabbing with a weapon? He and Daisy would make the thatcher their first call of the day.

Chapter Twenty-Two

Daisy drove Callum down the track to Crossways Farm and slowed as she went past the cobbled yard. The little Fiat, the Defender and the camper van were parked next to one another in a neat line below the house, but the black Jeep was missing.

'Probably doing the school run,' Daisy said, following Callum's line of thought.

They were passing the stables when Abigail appeared from one of the loose boxes pushing a wheelbarrow half-filled with straw. A long-handled fork was perched on top, and her gloved thumb held the shaft in place against the hand grip of the barrow. The two whippets dressed in their big-cat coats trotted out behind her and ears raised, looked across at their vehicle. Callum raised a hand to Abigail, who nodded her response as she guided her barrow along the concrete apron towards the next box.

Down in the barnyard, a vehicle was parked in front of each of the buildings. Penny was parked close to the stack of finished hurdles that leaned against the side of her barn. She had loaded half of these onto the bed of her pickup and was standing near the tailgate facing Keiron, both arms raised, flat palms towards the thatcher. He was standing too close to her, his stance aggressive, his forefinger prodding Penny in the chest. She had a surprised look on her face when he backed her up against the side of her vehicle. He only stopped walking when she was pressed against her pickup, unable to retreat any further, and his progress was impeded by her raised arms.

Daisy rolled to a stop and Callum lowered his window to catch what was being said.

'I know it was you,' Keiron shouted. 'It bloody well has to be, whatever you say.'

Callum opened the door and stepped away from the Navara. 'Is there a problem?' he asked.

'Not on my part,' Penny said quickly and ducked out from beneath Keiron's outstretched arms to put her vehicle between herself and the thatcher.

Keiron stabbed the empty air in her direction. 'You better give it back, Penny. Pronto.' He turned on his heel and yanked open the door of his vehicle, jumped in and gunned the engine. He slewed the pickup around, slammed shut his door and roared off up the track, peppering Callum and Penny with gravel.

'Are you okay?' Callum asked Penny. He heard Daisy get out of her vehicle behind him.

'Yes, I'm fine, thanks.' Penny straightened up the last hurdle she had loaded and turned her head to watch the retreating vehicle.

'What did I miss?' Daisy said, coming to stand beside Callum. 'Hi, Penny. I hear you're sponsoring a class at the gymkhana.'

Callum looked swiftly at Daisy. He did not want her going off-piste and would tell her so when they were alone. Then he realised why she had made her seemingly irrelevant comment. Penny's demeanour changed before his eyes. The tight muscles in her face relaxed and her shoulders, that had been raised, fell back to their normal place. Daisy was diffusing the tension, putting Penny at ease. His sergeant was very good at reading situations and was more empathetic to people's feelings than he was.

Callum thought she was sometimes oversensitive, but this time she was spot on.

Penny leaned back against the tailgate, folded her arms and smiled at Daisy. 'Yep. Under-twelves showjumping. I went for the under-twelves because I didn't want to sponsor a class that one of the Garland girls might win. They're all older than that, and it might have looked a bit embarrassing if I had to give them a trophy as I'm their tenant.'

'Are they good landlords?' Callum asked.

'Abi and George are the best. I couldn't wish for better,' Penny said.

'Just for a better neighbour?' Daisy laughed with a shake of her head.

'Got it in one. Still, beggars can't be choosers. I am lucky to have this barn and it's working out to be really good for business.'

'What was Keiron so wound up about?' Daisy asked.

'He's such hard work. He's lost some of his tools and has just accused me of stealing them. I told him that if he cleared up now and again, he would probably find them.'

'But you didn't take them?' Daisy said.

'Why would I? They're no good to me. They're probably in the garden of the last roof he did. I've seen him throwing tools down off the ridge to save having to climb up and down the ladder. He can't have any idea where they end up half the time.'

Daisy nodded towards the barn. 'They might be in there somewhere, hard to tell,' she said.

'That's exactly what I said to him, which is why he was standing shouting at me and telling me to mind my own business. Then he accused me of blaming him for losing them to cover the fact that I had stolen them from him.'

'Perhaps it's a case of the truth hurts,' Daisy said.

Penny huffed a breath. 'You're probably right. His dad came down here last week when Keiron was out. Mr Tapper wasn't best pleased with the state of the place, so I bet he had a go at him about tidying up and I just touched a nerve when I said if he put all his tools back where they lived, then he'd know where to find them.'

'Could be,' Daisy said.

Callum heard the doubt in Daisy's voice.

'You think differently?' he asked.

'Not really. I just think Keiron's not clearing up because his father said he should. He hated being told what to do when his dad was running the business. They were always at loggerheads.'

Callum thought that if there were constant disagreements between them, that was probably the reason that Tapper senior had not handed any control of the business to Keiron before his accident had forced him to do so.

'That's the problem with inherited businesses,' Penny said. 'Keiron has no idea how hard you have to work to get established when you first start out.'

'Did you start from scratch?' Callum asked.

'I did. Mum works in the chemist in Fordingbridge and Dad is a weaver at Wilton Carpet Factory. Noisy place. I just couldn't see myself stuck inside all the time. I like a bit of peace and quiet, me, and somehow, I ended up making hurdles and I love it.' Her phone buzzed in her pocket, and she took it out and checked the screen. 'My sister, Jen,' she said, 'sending me another picture of her new baby.' She slipped the mobile back in her pocket and Callum was grateful not to have to look at the photo.

'That reminds me,' Penny said. 'Jen and I had a run-in with Keiron in the supermarket car park a couple of weeks ago.'

'Why?' Callum asked.

'Because of his entitled attitude,' Penny said. 'He is such a pain in the bum. There weren't any empty mother-and-baby spaces, so we had to park in the ordinary ones. They're really close together and Jen struggles with her double buggy thingy. It takes about three times as long to go shopping with my nieces in tow.'

'I bet,' Daisy said. 'Go on.'

'Sod's law, when we walked past the mother-and-baby spaces to get to the shop entrance, one was free and Keiron pulled into it. There was a girl with him, too skinny with long blond hair, I think she's a friend of the Garlands. Anyway, they got out to go in the shop and Jen shouted after him, "Stop. You've forgotten your baby!" and all the shoppers looked round at them and some applauded Jen. The girl just laughed, bowed to the audience and then gave us the finger, but Keiron went red in the face. He had a go at me about it the next time I saw him. He thinks I put Jen up to it.'

'And did you?' Daisy asked with a smile.

'No, but I wish I had. It was damned funny.'

Penny had never seen Brendan come down to the yard and thought it unlikely that he was any relation to her family but offered to ask her mum and dad if either of them knew Brendan Stafford when she went to see them that night.

Chapter Twenty-Three

Walking back to the Navara, Daisy glanced up at the sky. 'It feels a bit warmer, and it looks like rain, don't you think, Callum?'

He did. The weather seemed to be taking no notice of the meteorologist's prediction of snow, but the wind was rising and biting his exposed flesh. When his phone pinged an incoming message, he slowed his pace to read it.

'Cookie confirms that Uniform visited Seb Wells this morning to check up on his guns,' Callum said. 'They were locked in the cabinet, exactly as he said they would be, surrounded by his dogs. They had to get him to put the dogs somewhere else because they were stopping the constables doing the check.'

'I didn't think there'd be any problem,' Daisy said as she zapped open her Navara. 'Poor Seb will be getting a complex. That's a phone call from Bird, then us seeing him at the pub and then a visit from Uniform.'

Callum's phone rang and he checked the caller as he climbed into the cab. It was Rain. He held the phone to his ear as Daisy drove onto the track heading towards the road. He looked out of the window at the furled brown beech leaves that were hanging onto the dry twigs of the hedge like sleeping bats.

‘Hi there.’ He could hear the smile in his own voice which caught him by surprise.

‘Cal, quick call; favour time, please.’

He could hear her footsteps on a hard surface and wondered if she was already at work.

‘How can I help?’ he asked. He was aware that Daisy had slowed her vehicle to a crawl, he thought, in an attempt to better hear his conversation.

‘Nothing drastic, but I should have asked you first.’

She seemed to be patting papers, and he knew then that she was still at the house and was probably looking for her car keys.

‘Tonight is my last shift for now and I have ordered some wool that should come later today, so it’s there when I’m off. I’ve all but finished that jumper I left at yours.’

Callum hoped that she was right, and that Amber had not created any lasting damage to the garment when she had tangled the yarns together. He heard a thunk, followed by the rattle of the letter box as she closed the door and then the traffic noise from the street.

‘Did you put down my address for delivery?’ he asked.

She laughed. It was a sudden, joyous sound that lifted his heart. ‘Too damn clever by half, you are,’ she said, still laughing. ‘Hope that was okay. I should have asked first.’

‘No problem. I wanted to ask you…’ He looked at Daisy’s reflection in the windscreen. Although her eyes were fixed on the road, her head was tilted to one side. ‘Maybe later. See you in the morning.’

‘I bet I can guess what it is. Bye, Cal. Miss you,’ Rain said softly.

He hesitated before speaking. ‘Ditto,’ he said and ended the call.

Yellow-dotted gorse bushes flashed past the window, frost-mantled and still looking cold, despite Daisy’s expectation of an increase in temperature. He wanted to hold onto the warmth of Rain’s laugh for a little longer, hug it to his heart and store the memory. He was surprised to find himself acknowledging how good it would feel to come home to her, to wake every morning with her sleeping next to him. He took a deep breath and slipped his phone back into his pocket.

He had thought more than once of asking Rain to move in with him, but he was concerned about putting pressure on her, unsure if he was moving their relationship along too quickly. He liked what they had and was scared that changing the status quo would spoil it. Was it too soon to broach the subject? Was it what Rain wanted? With a jolt of surprise, he realised that it was very much what he wanted.

Daisy flicked a look at him, an impish grin on her face. She looked back to road and took a breath.

'Don't,' Callum said, before she had the chance to speak.

'Spoilsport,' she muttered, smiling.

* * *

Callum stood beside the board that stretched across part of the back wall of the office and the other members of his team gathered around him. Daisy and Legs stood side by side, their height disparity making Callum think of a duo in a comedy sketch. Bird leaned against the edge of a desk, arms folded across his chest, his head turned towards Cookie who stood next to him, rocking backwards and forwards, heel to toe, heel to toe.

Callum pointed to an empty chair. 'Cookie, have a seat, please. Where are we with these burglaries?'

'No new activity reported today, and nothing last night.' Cookie's curls bounced. 'The last one reported was the Pearsons, when the "yow" was out.' He laughed at his rural pronunciation but stopped abruptly when Bird looked at him.

Callum turned to Bird. 'Any positive responses from pawn shops?'

'Nothing, guv.' Bird shook his head. 'We checked Bournemouth and Southampton, the closest two opportunities to get rid of stuff, but nobody has issued a pledge agreement for any of the distinctive pieces of jewellery or bought them outright. And no one is admitting to seeing that pricey watch of Bellman's golfing mate's.'

'Wouldn't they just send it up to Birmingham or Hatton Garden for smelting?' Cookie asked. 'That'd be the quickest way to get some money back, wouldn't it?'

'Quick, yeah,' Bird said. 'But that wouldn't get them the best price. These burglars have got an eye for quality; they only lifted the really good stuff. They left behind the run-of-the-mill gear.' He unfolded his arms. 'Some of those heirloom bits won't fetch much if you melt them down because they only pay on the weight of the gold. They don't pay anything for the weight of the stones. It'd benefit them to hang onto the stuff for a bit and then sell them as pieces, not scrap. They'll get more for them that way.'

'I suppose so,' Cookie said, and began tapping his heel against his chair leg. 'I did check with the local post office in case. They would have had to post it insured because of the value, but they hadn't had anything like that through.'

'Good thought, Cookie,' Callum said. 'It was worth checking.' Callum addressed them all. 'Something has changed if the burglaries have stopped. What? Keep that in mind. Now, Brendan Stafford. Update please.'

Bird reached for a sheet of paper from the desk next to him. 'I'm still waiting for that solicitor, guv, the one who did the will and promised to come back to me. I've phoned twice already today but she's always with a client.' He frowned and scrubbed a flat hand over his tufted hair. 'I reckon they do it on purpose, bleedin' drag things out, just so they can charge the customer a bigger bill.' He looked around at all the eyes fixed on his face. 'Just saying.' He grinned. 'Getting off me soap box now.'

'Keep trying,' Callum said. He updated them on his conversations with Penny Hopwood and Susie Treadwell. 'Keiron seems to have a very short fuse, and we now know he argued with Brendan, which gives us a possible connection between Brendan and Keiron. Did they know each other before Brendan came down here house-hunting? Cookie, take a look at both of their phone records. See if they have been in contact with one another recently, or before Brendan came to our neck of the woods. He still could be the reason for the relocation.'

'Okey-dokey.' Cookie shot to his feet.

'And you were checking his search history,' Callum continued. 'Anything?'

'Nothing,' Cookie said sitting back down. 'He doesn't have a history of visiting porn sites.' He counted the points off on his fingers as he spoke. 'Nothing about grooming kids or a paedophile connection, unless he had another laptop stashed somewhere else that we don't know about, but there's nothing on his cloud, and no dark web stuff. Perhaps it's a new hobby for retirement.'

'I've heard more far-fetched theories, Cookie,' Bird said, shaking his head, his expression disapproving, 'but not this side of the Millenium.'

Callum agreed but made no comment. Cookie was very skilled at retrieving information from electronic devices when users were confident it was invisibly hidden. He was equally skilled at inventing theories when he was short of concrete facts.

'Legs, you were chasing up Forensics. Any joy?' Callum asked.

Legs shook her head. 'I was hoping for something from his clothes that would give us an idea of where he was attacked. There was nothing we can work with, no cross-contamination, no fibres and no plant matter, just gravel.'

'That's no help,' Daisy said. 'His car was parked on gravel, the pub parking is on gravel, so is the village hall and so are about ninety percent of people's driveways round here. Absolutely nothing else to go on?'

'Nothing,' Legs said. 'And they have searched the cricket pitch area and the village hall and there is still no sign of the murder weapon, or his keys, or his phone.'

Searching every gravel space in the village was not an option in terms of both time and manpower. Callum was disappointed not to have found a connection between Brendan and someone local. That would have increased their chance of finding out where the attack took place and of locating the weapon used to murder Brendan. The link between the thatcher and the victim was tenuous at best, but it was all they had.

'Daisy and I will go and have a word at the Drunken Donkey,' Callum said. 'There's a possibility that the staff know what the aggravation between Keiron and Brendan was about.'

He went into the fishbowl for his jacket. Daisy pushed her arms into the sleeves of her coat and waited for him at the office door.

Chapter Twenty-Four

The blue-and-white camper van was still parked next to the fence of the Drunken Donkey and Daisy pulled up next to it.

'Do you reckon they've died of frostbite and nobody has noticed?' she asked as she nodded at the vehicle and switched off her engine.

'I don't think frostbite in itself is fatal,' Callum said and opened the wicket gate for Daisy to proceed him to the pub door.

Picnic tables dotted the grass of the pub garden and were enclosed behind a paling fence. Callum imagined that on a warm summer's day, al fresco drinking and dining was a big draw for the pub. The fence around the eating area was probably there to stop ponies and donkeys encroaching on the customers. Currently, all the tables were rimed with frost and empty except for a hopeful robin. He hopped about, his plumage puffed out by the insulating warm air trapped beneath his feathers.

'Lucky for me then.' She pulled open the half-glazed door and they walked into the carpeted warmth.

There were people eating at tables and their chatter was underpinned by popular music tracks from, Callum thought, the 1970s or 80s. He followed Daisy to the bar that was manned by two young women, both wearing black shirts logoed on the left side with the name of the establishment above an embroidered lop-eared donkey.

When Callum introduced himself and Daisy, one of the women left through a door at the rear of the bar and returned a few moments later with a man dressed in green moleskin trousers and a checked shirt who announced himself as Finn Lewis, the manager. He was drying his hands on a brown towel and when he had finished, he passed it to one of the women.

'Helping prep veg,' he said. 'What can I do for you?'

His shirtsleeves were folded back, exposing his forearms, the muscles flexing as he smoothed flat a ruckled towelling mat on the bar top. Callum glimpsed a heavy buckle ring on his finger before Finn pushed his hands into the pockets of his sleeveless fleece.

The manager hadn't seen the argument between Brendan and Keiron but had heard the talk about it in the bar afterwards. Keiron had been suspicious that Brendan had dented the door of his pickup and wouldn't let it rest despite having no evidence.

'He's like a dog with a bone, that one,' Finn said. 'He wouldn't let it go. The lads said that Keiron failed to get a rise out of the chap, despite goading him, and the calmer he stayed, the more het-up Keiron got. The bloke finished his drink and walked out and Keiron just about exploded and followed him outside. If I'd been behind the bar, I'd have told Keiron to pull his neck in. That sort of thing is bad for business.'

'Do you know the other man?' Callum asked.

'No. The girls tell me he's been in here for his supper a few times recently and that he's looking to move to the village.'

'Chatty sort, then?' Daisy said.

Finn glanced across at one of the young women behind the bar, who was smiling as she handed a drink to a customer. 'Not necessarily,' he said. 'Tess there could prise the fillings out of your teeth when your mouth was closed. She told me he was house-hunting. I think she was a bit disappointed that she couldn't find out much else about him.'

Finn looked around at the sound of a door opening at the rear of the bar. The door was marked "private". Two Irish wolfhounds trotted out and went straight towards Daisy who barely had to stoop down to fuss the tall dogs. They were followed into the bar by a woman wearing a knee-length red down coat, and a grey fur hat with two dog leads looped around her neck. She fumbled her hands into mittens and called to Finn as she headed for the outer door.

'We'll be about half an hour. Don't forget to call the veggie man.'

Callum saw Daisy move across the bar and speak to the woman before both she and her dogs exited. Daisy closed the door after them and came back to perch on a bar stool at Callum's elbow.

'How do you get along with Keiron?' Callum asked Finn.

'He's one that spends most of his evenings in here. Probably stalling going home. Joe, that's his dad, comes in at lunchtimes and things are a bit rocky between them at the moment, reading between the lines.'

'Because?' Callum said.

'Because Keiron is pig-headed and angry and won't take any notice of what his old man says. It's six of one and half a dozen of the other though, if you ask me. Keiron wants to do it his way, which isn't Joe's way.'

'And Joe is not happy,' Callum said. 'But you get along with Keiron?'

'More or less.' Finn called a 'thank you' to a departing customer. 'If Keiron put as much effort into the business as he does bad-mouthing Joe, we'd all stop getting earache from the pair of them.'

'It can be difficult working with family,' Daisy said and flicked a sideways glance at Callum.

Her brother was working overseas and her parents worked and lived in France, so Callum knew it was not a personal observation but rather that she was encouraging the landlord to expand his comments.

'Depends on what you're made of,' Finn said. 'Take young Eddie. His father led him a merry dance when he was alive and Eddie was always having to bail him out of this problem and that, but he won't hear a word said against his old man.'

The corner of Daisy's mouth lifted. 'Does Eddie come in here much?'

Finn hesitated before answering. 'Now and again. Never on his own and always sits near the door.' He looked Callum in the eye. 'He's allergic to alcohol.'

Callum nodded his understanding. In his trade Finn must come across many who had an unhealthy relationship with drink.

'I've got a lot of time for Eddie,' Finn said. 'Excuse me a sec. Duty calls.' He turned to a man standing at the bar. 'Yes, sir, what can I get you?' Finn reached a glass from a shelf, filled it with a soft drink and passed it across the counter. He turned back to Callum. 'Is there anything else I can help you with, Inspector?'

'That's all for now. Thanks for your time,' Callum said and followed Daisy to the door.

They walked past the camper van and Daisy nodded at it.

'Two lads,' Daisy said, as they got into her Navara. 'This is their last night here. They were supposed to be going skiing this week, but they went to a stag do last weekend. One broke his ankle and the other one his wrist. God knows what they were doing. So, they changed plans, borrowed a camper van and came to the New Forest instead. Stella told me.'

Callum wondered which one of them was driving. He correctly assumed Stella to be the woman with the enormous hairy dogs that Daisy had spoken to in the bar.

'She's the landlady. And she told me something else.' Daisy paused, her tyres once again sinking into the two water-filled ruts before she pulled out onto the road to drive through Godshill village. 'She thinks Eddie's ex Lucy is a bit too friendly with Keiron.'

'Being friendly with someone is not yet against the law. Drive on,' Callum said.

He looked out of the passenger window. Grey gorse bushes dotted with yellow flowers crawled past. Bent bracken beneath the spikey branches was still pale with frost and the puddled ruts in the tracks were rimed white with ice. He watched a couple with a small child. He, or she, was bundled into a padded hood-to-toe suit patterned with dinosaurs. The parents watched as the child jumped green frog wellington boots up and down on the same spot until they broke through the icy covering to splash into the puddle hiding beneath.

Callum's mind chased connections, between Keiron and Lucy, between Keiron and Penny, and between Keiron and Brendan. He just had to jump on the right puddle to break through the ice and find the connection he was seeking. The child tripped and fell, and the mother scooped it up and hugged it to her. Callum looked forward through the windscreen at the ribbon of grey that dipped and turned then rose and straightened guiding them into the future.

He had been thinking about his own future. Thoughts and ideas were circling around in his head like a carousel. But every time it stopped, he put off making a decision and set the wheel in motion once again. For the last five days it had stopped again and again at the same place. Now, he sat a little taller in his seat, and his chest fluttered against his seat belt. He would ask Rain to move in with him. The worst that could happen was that she would say no. He tucked his hair back behind his ear and felt Daisy turn her head to sneak a glance at him.

'All right, sir?' She lifted her foot from the accelerator.

'Very,' he said. 'Stop dawdling.'

They slowed to cross the second of the two single-width bridges at Breamore Mill. A pickup had pulled to the side of the road and waited for them to clear the brick-sided structure so it could proceed.

'Jimmy,' Daisy said, nodding at the waiting vehicle.

'Pull in,' Callum said, pointing to the gravel track leading off at a tangent from the bend in the road. 'I want a quick word with him.'

The river that ran alongside the road before disappearing under the bridge was wide and filled with weeds, its surface black and shiny. Chilled air rose from the water, and Callum breathed in the strong smell of damp vegetation as he crossed the tarmac to the waiting pickup. The scent reminded him of the winter breath of kale-fed cattle at his grandparents' croft on Seil Island. The water churned and rushed through the mill race, throwing a damp mist upwards and it hung in the air like an opaque cloud. It touched his cheeks and made him shiver. Daisy waited in her car. Jimmy lowered his window as Callum approached and the piebald collie on the passenger seat stood and wagged her tail in greeting.

'Afternoon, Jimmy. Thanks for stopping,' Callum said, and reached his hand through the open window to stroke the dog's head.

'Enough, Panda, now sit. No problem,' Jimmy said. 'What do you want to know?'

Callum acknowledged that he often approached people because he was seeking information and grinned. 'Where would I take a deer carcass if I wanted to sell it?'

Jimmy huffed a laugh. 'I assume you mean without paperwork. Harry Kingman's your man for butchering; I can't speak for him when it comes to paperwork.' He raised his window and drove slowly over the bridge towards Woodgreen.

Chapter Twenty-Five

Callum got back into Daisy's car.

She pulled off the verge onto the road before speaking. 'I forgot to say that Sue Eastwood told me last night that Jimmy has managed to find a new pony that might suit Flissa Garland. She's going to have it on trial. Did Jimmy say?'

'He did not. Slow down.' Ahead Callum saw that a stationary pickup was facing them and partially blocking their side of the lane ahead of them. When they got closer, he recognised Penny Hopwood standing at the rear of her vehicle. She was offloading hurdles, hefting them up to balance on her shoulder before carrying them through a narrow wicket gate. She disappeared behind an evergreen hedge, before shortly reappearing without the hurdle.

Presumably she heard Daisy's car approaching when she made her return journey through the gate empty-handed. She looked in their direction and signalled to them to stop. Daisy pulled in behind the parked pickup and Callum got out.

'Glad I caught you,' Penny said.

She lifted the last remaining hurdle from her vehicle and placed it on the ground next to her. The split hazel rods were woven around firm uprights and then tamped down to form a rigid, self-supporting panel. He was about to ask Penny why she had left a small empty square section midway up the four-foot-tall structure, when she pushed her hand through the opening and grasped the hurdle through the gap. Callum realised that it was a purpose-made hole to assist in carrying the unwieldy panels with greater ease. She lifted it a foot off the ground and walked it towards the open gate.

'The homeowners have got a new puppy, and he's gorgeous. They're going to use some of my hurdles to make a temporary enclosure on the lawn at the back of the house. He's so little that he could get through their hedges. When he's a bit bigger, they will just use the hurdles to reinforce the fences round the outside of the garden.' She went through the gate.

Callum waited for her to return. The leaves of the hedge shimmered, and he assumed that she was leaning the hurdle against the other side. She returned to join him, closing the gate behind her.

'That's me finished here.' She slipped off her red rubberised gloves and pushed them into the pocket of her fleece.

'You wanted to see me?' Callum said.

'Yes. I asked Mum and Dad last night if they knew Brendan Stafford. I thought perhaps they might have gone to school with him if he came from round here, because of his age.'

'And did they know him?' Out of the corner of his eye, he saw Daisy get out of her vehicle and walk towards them.

'No. They'd never heard of him before he died. And they don't remember any local family with that surname either. Sorry.'

'Thanks for checking.'

Callum heard Daisy call hello to someone behind him and turned to see her speaking to the Palmer brothers through the open driver's window of their camper van. They had pulled tight to the side of the road behind them and stopped as a tractor and flat-bed trailer loaded with hay bales growled past. The driver, an overall-dressed man wearing a baseball cap, inched through the narrow gap between the vehicles and the white railings that sided the River Avon. A waft of herby grass and diesel fumes billowed in his wake.

Penny raised her hand to the tractor driver. 'That's going to the Garlands. I said I'd help the girls unload, so I'd better get my skates on.'

'I'll let you get on then,' Callum said.

Penny lifted the tailgate of her pickup and fastened it in place. 'That does mean that Brendan wasn't looking for me if he was down by our barns, so he must have been looking for Keiron.'

'That seems likely to be the case. One more thing, the girl you and your sister saw Keiron with at the supermarket when you were parking your car, why did you think she was a friend of the Garlands?'

'Because when I came back to the barn one afternoon – last week, I think it was – she was walking out of the drive onto Roger Penny Way. Must dash. Bye now.' Penny checked again that the tailgate was secure by rattling it against the fastenings then got into her pickup, pulled out around the Navara and drove back towards Woodgreen. Behind them the camper van quietly overtook them and pulled away, heading in the opposite direction.

Daisy appeared at his elbow. 'Ready?' she asked. 'That was the Palmers,' she said, unnecessarily. 'They're going to look for migratory birds down on Breamore Marsh.'

They got back into her vehicle.

'I want to call in at Kingman's,' Callum said as she pulled away from the verge.

'Okay.' She changed up a gear. 'Tom is quite pleasant to talk to; bit of a charmer, really,' Daisy said. 'He was smiley and jokey, but the other brother, Mickey, is a total misery. I never noticed before, but he's got a nasty scar – an old one – down the side of his face. He never said a word the whole time I was talking to Tom. Just looked daggers at us both.'

'What did Tom have to say?'

'Not much really, but he didn't let Mickey get a word in edgeways. He was just killing time while he waited for the tractor and trailer. He told me what birds they had been looking for and that Mickey fell and hurt his leg a couple of days ago climbing down a bank, so they've been taking it easy. That's why they're going to the marsh, because they can see most of it without getting out of their vehicle. They're off down to the coast tomorrow, Christchurch way, looking for winter-visiting seabirds.'

Callum remembered Mickey staggering when he got out of the camper van in the Garlands' cobbled yard and cannoning against the side of the vehicle. He had assumed that the man had been drinking. Perhaps he had done him an injustice if he had in fact taken a tumble and his leg was hurting him.

* * *

The fields Callum saw through the window were mostly green, but frost still lingered beneath the hedgerows as if the ground was dusted with icing sugar. The tramlines across the fields made by the tractor wheels were brown parallel grooves that textured the pasture like napped corduroy. In the deepest of these ruts, water wallowed, mirrors of the grey, heavy sky.

'What's in that field?' Callum asked Daisy as they drove past another area. An electric fence divided the crop. One side was green, and undisturbed, the other was brown and puddled by a flock of sheep.

'Sheep,' Daisy said taking a quick look.

Callum inhaled a noisy breath. She was being obtuse. He knew what sheep looked like.

'Strip grazing turnips, by the look of it,' she added with an impish grin.

Callum wondered how many of the animals would end up in Kingman's shop inside the fish tank counter display.

Chapter Twenty-Six

Harry Kingman was serving a customer when Callum and Daisy went into the shop. The bell above the door had barely finished its tinny peal before Irene appeared from the back room, a pencil in her hand, and asked how she could help them. When Callum said they wanted a word with Harry she nodded, put the pencil behind her ear and set about tidying the stack of paper behind the counter that Harry used for wrapping purchases. She made no attempt to engage the officers in conversation, but did flash a glance at Harry.

While he was waiting, Callum looked at the meat on display. The venison looked good, and he thought perhaps he would buy some and cook a special meal for Rain tomorrow evening, hopefully to celebrate her accepting his offer to move into Hope Cottage with him. He realised that he didn't know if she liked venison. He frowned – perhaps he should play safe and buy steak.

'Can I help?' Harry's voice broke into Callum's thoughts, followed by the graunch of the door closing behind the departing customer.

'I'm sure you can,' Callum said. 'Where do you get your venison from?'

He had kept his tone relaxed but Irene swung round to face them. The pencil flew from behind her ear and clattered onto the tiled floor between her and Harry.

'Goodness sake, woman,' Harry said and watched her pick it up before answering the question. 'Various people. All legit. You don't need to worry about that.' He puffed out his apron-covered chest and wiped his fingers down the front.

Callum had not been worrying about it until Harry told him not to. 'Anyone in particular?' he asked.

'Various hunters. And before you ask, they're all members of the National Gamekeepers' Organisation.' He pointed to a red-covered book on a shelf behind the till. 'All in there. Names, tag numbers, dates. All the details, and they are checked regularly by them that needs to know.' He paused and seemed to be deciding if he should elaborate. 'The EHO, the environmental health officer, that is,' he added as an afterthought.

Callum waited. He heard Daisy's boot soles scuff on the floor as she fidgeted beside him.

Then Harry said, 'Come and see for yourself.' He gestured to Irene who lifted up a hinged section of the counter then stood to one side to give the officers access.

They followed Harry through a doorway into the back of the property. Callum was surprised to find that it was one large room with an oversized stainless-steel table in the middle of the tiled floor and a similar counter that snaked around the walls. Chopping boards were placed at intervals along the surface, which was dotted with an assortment of saws, knives and other sundry equipment. Despite it being cool in the room, the smells of warm blood and disinfectant mingled, reminding Callum of his initial meeting with the butcher in the village hall.

A half-glazed door at the far end of the room led out into a brick-paved yard with a single-storey building on one side.

'In my old man's time that building there was an abattoir. We stopped using it back in the sixties – too many rules and regulations to comply with. It wasn't viable with all the new conditions they kept imposing on us. I converted it to a game larder.'

Harry moved towards a gap in the worktops that allowed space for a shiny steel door in the wall. There was a light switch beside the jamb. He pulled on the large handle, and the door swung towards him and then banged against the side of the steel bench with the clang of metal on metal. Harry flicked the light switch and dangling fluorescent tubes hummed into life except for the one just inside the door, which buzzed like a trapped wasp, then fell silent. It did this a couple of times before bursting into life and lighting the space inside the store.

Cold air swirled out of the door and chilled Callum's face. Beside him, Daisy shivered. Sundry carcasses hung in the room, suspended from hooks dangling from the ceiling. The closest was a deer, the brown hide still in place but minus the head and lower legs. It was hanging by a hind leg. Harry reached out, pulled the meat towards them and swivelled it around to show the ribcage and the empty cavity of the chest. Close up it didn't smell as strongly as Callum had imagined that it would.

'Irene washes out the cavity with salt water. Reduces the taint,' Harry said. He took hold of a white label that was threaded through the hind leg in the gap between the tendon and the muscle.

'See? That tells me what it was, and when it was killed.' He turned the label to show the reverse. 'And that's the hunter's ID number and his name. All legit and above board.' Harry propelled the carcass back into the cold store with a push, clicked closed the door and switched off the lights.

'So that was a fallow deer, killed early this morning by S Wells?' Callum said. Being killed so recently would account for the drops of blood he had noticed that had dripped from the beast onto the floor beneath it.

'That's right, a buck. You can't shoot a deer between sunset and sunrise. He's a skilled hunter, good marksman, clean headshot. Some of them kill with a body shot because it's a bigger target but it damages the meat so I can't pay them as much. I'll hang it for four or five days, then butcher it into primal cuts and leave it in there on the shelf for a bit longer.' Harry moved to wipe his hands down the front of his apron again but stopped himself and went across the room to wash them in the sink.

'Why do you leave the skin on?' Daisy asked. 'All the others in there looked as if they had been skinned.'

Harry flicked droplets of water from his fingers, and they splashed up the tiles behind the sink. 'The others aren't deer and in my humble opinion, if you leave the coat on, it stops the venison drying out while it's hanging. And you leave it to hang so that the enzymes in the meat break down the fibres and that improves the texture and flavour.' He pulled two blue paper towels from a dispenser and dried his hands. 'That's why supermarket meat has no flavour. It costs time and money to hang it, and they want it shifted before it's ready.' He bunched the damp paper towels into a wadge and threw them into the sink.

Harry went back into the shop and ushered them out through the gap in the counter. 'So, if you want meat with any flavour, you can't do better than Kingman's because we do a proper job and don't put profit before the customer.' He grinned and folded his arms across his chest.

Irene paused in her wiping-down of the shop counter then recommenced her activity with increased effort.

Callum took his wallet from his pocket then pointed a finger at a beef sirloin. 'Can you cut me a couple of steaks, please?'

'Good choice. That steer came from a farm just up the road. An Aberdeen Angus.' Harry removed the joint from the display and placed onto the steel table behind the counter. He used a long-bladed knife to deftly cut off two steaks, holding them up for Callum to nod his approval. Then Harry weighed and wrapped them, sliding Irene's recently tidied paper stack into disarray. He keyed information into a handheld reader and lifted it towards Callum for him to tap his card against it.

'You wouldn't buy from someone who doesn't have a Gamekeepers' ID card, like Eddie Gilligan, for instance?' asked Callum.

Harry's hand hovered in mid-air for a second before he completed the action of passing Callum his purchase. Irene snatched a swift look at Harry before going out into the back room.

'Absolutely not. No tag, no purchase.'

* * *

'Special occasion?' Daisy said, nodding to the wrapped steak. She paused, her finger above the ignition button, and when Callum didn't answer, she gave a shallow shrug and started the engine. 'I'll take that as a yes, then, shall I?'

Chapter Twenty-Seven

They were nearly back to the station when Callum saw a green-painted wooden sign sitting askew on top of a staddle stone and leaning against a holly hedge. It was at the entrance to a track leading off the road on their left.

Joe Tapper – Thatcher.

Keiron was still using the signs that his father had made when he had run the business.

Callum pointed towards it. 'Turn down that track,' he said.

The tall holly hedge on one side and yew bushes on the other shut out the light and Daisy's automatic headlights came on. 'Spooky,' she said.

The greenery on Daisy's side gave way to a post and rail fence beyond which were wide flat lawns surrounding a chocolate-box cottage. They turned off the track and onto the driveway of the property just as Keiron began descending a long ladder that rested against a newly re-thatched straw roof. The ridge covering was scallop-edged and decorated with an intricate pattern formed by criss-crossing hazel liggers. Two straw finials were attached to the ridge, a fox at one end and a chicken at the other. Callum thought the thatch looked neat and attractive.

Evidently the work of a skilled craftsman despite the craftsman in question having an argumentative disposition.

A red gorilla tub, a handled, soft-sided plastic container favoured by workmen, sat close to the foot of the ladder. Keiron stepped off the bottom rung, tossed a tool into the tub, where it landed with the chink of metal on metal.

'I'm finished here. Just packing up,' he said to the detectives and moved towards the white cob wall of the cottage. He stirred the lavender shrubs with a booted foot, then bent forward to lift a reed needle from within the grey stalks and pitch it into the tub.

'I wanted to ask you about Brendan Stafford,' Callum said.

Keiron stilled for a second then carried on picking up tools. 'The only aggro I had with him was him driving into my pickup truck and then denying he did it.'

Keiron's vehicle was reversed up close to the wall of the cottage. An opened bundle of straw had spread across the flat bed of the pickup and the musky dust floated towards the detectives. His tools still in his hand, Keiron walked to the passenger side of his vehicle.

'See?' He pointed with his toe to a dent at the bottom of the passenger door. 'That's where he hit it. He said he didn't, but I know he did. Poncey prick.' He returned to the red tub in the flower border, dropped the tools he was holding into it and then hefted the tub up onto the bed of the pickup, rustling the scattered straw.

'When did you see him last?' Callum asked.

'Probably that day I had the upper and downer with him. I didn't do him in, if that's what you're thinking.' Keiron walked back to the cottage. The muscles across his shoulders bunched beneath his T-shirt when he reached up to grasp the rungs of the ladder and lift it away from the new thatch.

'Did he come down to the barns to speak to you?' Daisy said.

'Nope. Why would he?' Keiron answered without hesitation. He lifted the rung locks and slid the extended section towards the feet, halving the height of the ladder.

'He's not a relative of yours, then?' Callum asked.

Keiron barked a short laugh. 'We've got enough poncey pricks in our family as it is. We don't need another one.'

'Did you find the missing tools that you thought Penny had taken?' Callum asked.

'Most of them,' Keiron said. 'I'm still missing a reeding pin and a knife and whatever she says, Penny is the only one who could of took them.'

'What's a reeding pin?' Callum asked.

Keiron reached into the back of his pickup and lifted a length of thin metal with a T-bar across the top. 'Reeding pin, set pin, whatever. You use it to shove down into the thatch and build up the straw until it's the height of the bar to make sure it's the same depth all over the roof. Different depths for different jobs. Ridge thatch is deeper.' He tossed the pin back into the pickup. 'The one that's been nicked is part of a set that belongs to the old man. He'll go ape if he knows it's missing.'

The detectives stood next to Daisy's Navara and watched Keiron pick up the last of his belongings and equipment from the lavender beds and surrounding gravel. Penny was correct. He was a careless operator.

'Might Lucy have taken it on one of her visits?' Callum said, feeling Daisy's shoulder brush his arm as she suddenly looked up at him.

Keiron flushed and snapped his head round to face Callum. 'Who told you about that? It wasn't my fault. She made all the running.' He removed his gloves and threw them into the back of his vehicle where they landed, one in the bucket and the other in the loose straw.

Callum remained still and quiet but felt Daisy glance up at him again. He placed a cautioning finger on her arm. He did not want her to speak. He wanted Keiron to comment on the situation unprompted.

'Anyway' – Keiron forcefully slammed closed the tailgate of his vehicle – 'it's ended. Happy now?'

'But you were seeing her when she was engaged to Eddie?' Callum asked.

'She was seeing me, more like. You done with me?' Without waiting for an answer, he got in his cab and drove away, his tyres spitting gravel into the lavender border.

'How did you know?' Daisy asked, a tinge of accusation in her tone.

'I didn't. It was just a lucky guess.' He watched the pickup turn onto the lane with barely a flicker of brake lights. 'From Penny's description of the girl's behaviour at the supermarket, she didn't seem to be a person that Abigail would encourage as a friend for her daughters. Penny didn't know her, so she had to be visiting Keiron. I can't see Lucy as a friend of the Garland girls. Can you?'

They got back in the Navara.

'I don't see her as a friend of anybody, now you ask,' Daisy said. 'And it answers a few questions.'

'Such as?' Callum snapped closed his seat belt.

'Such as who lived close enough for that impromptu liaison Lucy went off to after the baby shower.' She drove out into the lane. 'Such as a reason for Keiron having a bed on the tallet.'

'Maybe,' he said.

'And Seb saying she had been with someone and walked back to the Donkey afterwards, so it had to be very local.'

'Lucy doesn't have a car. Your theory could be correct.'

'Keiron and Lucy deserve each other, if you ask me,' Daisy said as she turned into the station.

Chapter Twenty-Eight

Callum pushed the door open and waited for Daisy to catch up with him and precede him into the office. Legs looked up, her box braids swirling. Cookie swayed from side to side on his chair, chewing in time with his body movements, a chocolate wrapper on his desktop beside his keyboard.

Bird forcefully scribbled a pen in tight circles in the margin of a sheet of paper. 'Useless piece of crap,' he said before tossing the item into his waste bin. He had all the patience in the world with the injured birds that he and his partner Helen rehabilitated. Pens did not receive the same consideration. He looked up as Callum reached his desk.

'Guv, I got hold of that solicitor at last,' Bird said. 'She's been snowed under. Their firm's staffing figures are worse than ours.'

'And that's saying something,' Daisy said coming to join the men.

'And?' Callum was not about to get lured into a discussion about something he was powerless to change.

'And Brendan did change his will. It was all going to his wife before the divorce, but now it is split equally between Charlotte Lauren Dunn and Darcie Holly Dunn. Are you thinking what I'm thinking?' Bird said, looking up at Callum.

'I'm thinking,' Daisy said, 'that it's too much of a coincidence that the two oldest Garland girls have the same Christian names as the beneficiaries.'

Legs had obviously been listening to their conversation, as she left her desk to come and join them.

'But Abigail said she didn't know him,' Legs said.

'Well, I reckon Abigail Garland is telling porkies, and she was one of his conquests,' Bird said. 'What do you reckon, guv?'

'It's a fair assumption.' Callum took a moment to review the information they currently had about Brendan's life, and it fitted neatly with the team's supposition. He caught a sudden movement in his peripheral vision and Cookie scooted across the room to join the rest of the team.

'Let's verify a few facts before we get carried away,' Callum said. 'Cookie, find the birth certificates for Charlotte and Darcie Garland and see if there's any connection with Charlotte and Darcie Dunn. Who are the parents shown on the certificates?'

'Hunky-doodley, guv.' Cookie bounced from foot to foot, making his corkscrew curls dance and his piano-key tie ripple as if it was being caressed by a concert pianist.

'And find the marriage certificate for Abigail and George.' Callum stared at Cookie as if looking at him would still the restless detective. 'What was her maiden name; where and when were they married?' Callum widened his focus to encompass the rest of the team. 'If we are on the right track, and Brendan is the father of the oldest two daughters, when were their names changed? Perhaps George adopted them. Find out. I want all the facts before we go any further with this.'

'Couldn't we just go and ask Abigail for all the details?' Legs asked.

'Let's not put the cart before the horse. There are children to consider here, and I want those questions answered before we do anything else. Let's verify the facts before we approach the Garlands. Understood?'

'Got it,' Bird said, turning his attention to his computer.

'Yes, siree,' Cookie said over his shoulder as he raced back to his desk.

The two women didn't move.

'Assuming we are right about this,' Legs said, 'do you think that Brendan came here looking for the girls themselves?'

'It's too much of a coincidence for it to be anything else,' Daisy said. 'What I'd like to know is what he was planning to do when he found them.'

'Apart from taking their photos,' Callum said. 'Daisy, did you believe Abigail when she said that she didn't recognise Brendan?'

Daisy stirred the toe of her boot against the floor while she considered his question.

'I did believe her. She was a bit nervy, but at the time I felt she was telling us the truth when we spoke to her. Now I'm not so sure. But she doesn't come across as the sort of person who uses knuckledusters and stabs people.'

Callum agreed with her assessment but having forged a possible connection between Abigail and Brendan, he couldn't ignore it. If Abigail had lied about knowing him, she could also have lied about seeing him. Had she perceived him as a threat to her family? If she had, it gave Abigail a motive to make sure that, whatever his plans were, Brendan didn't succeed.

* * *

The yellow plastic-wrapped parcel on his doorstep was larger than he imagined it would be to contain a few balls of yarn. He took hold of Rain's package with the same hand that held his own bag. With the other, he turned the key in the lock and elbowed open his front door. Before he could reach out with his foot to close the door, Amber flashed through the gap and out into the dark.

Callum dropped his belongings around him and rushed outside. Daisy had cautioned him to keep the cat indoors for at least four weeks until she learned that this was her new home. He hurried down the path towards his gate, but there was no sign of the animal. He went around the side of the house and, using the torch on his phone, searched for her in the apple orchard. The trees were old and bent and made grotesque shapes in the bright beam of light. He called her name, and his frosted breath hung in the air in front of him. At the far end of the orchard orange eyes glinted, paused for a second before disappearing. Amber's eyes reflected yellow. He hoped that the fox would not consider his cat as supper.

Fifteen minutes later, his search proving fruitless, he went back inside. He filled her bowl with food and unlocked the cat flap. If Daisy was just being pessimistic, and Amber could find her way back home, he wanted to make sure she could get into the house.

After supper he put on his jacket, slipped a torch into his pocket, and walked back to his previous cottage alongside Hatchet Green. In the absence of traffic and street lights, his eyes soon became accustomed to the darkness. He walked down the centre of Tethering Drove, his footfalls sounding like some distant drum. Lights inside the ribbon of houses on his right spilled out into gardens or peeped between drawn curtains. He stopped near the bottom of the drove and called 'Amber'. He waited for a moment, hoping for a responding miaow but all he heard was the growl of a distant vehicle and a bird-like fluttering in the bushes that edged the field to his left.

He walked over the crossroads towards the village green. The naked oak trees arched over his head, the bare branches squeaking against one another. He stepped on a twig and the crack sounded like a pistol shot in the dark.

At the top of the green he paused again, called her name and listened. A groan of breath and a grunt beside him had him reaching for his torch. He swung around and detected a feral, ammonia scent. Three shaggy-coated black cows stood together, jaws moving rhythmically as they chewed the cud. A curl of steam rising from a cowpat disappeared into the chill air. He put the torch back in his pocket and walked on towards his old home. Passing his previous neighbour, an extractor fan hummed into life, and the pungent smell of frying onions accompanied him for the final paces.

He clicked open the cottage gate. His lease did not expire until the end of the week, so there were no lights on inside the property and no car parked outside. He walked along the path to the back door and nudged the cat flap with his toe. It was locked, which was how he had left it. No chance that Amber could regain entry.

'Amber,' he called softly, but no grey shadow separated itself from the bushes and came to greet him. He walked around the rear garden, shining his torch beam beneath shrubs and into the leafless silver birch tree, but there was no sign of the cat.

He toyed with the idea of opening the cat flap but decided against it. He would come back in the morning to check if she was sitting on the doorstep. If she wasn't there, he would leave a note for Rain explaining what had happened so that she didn't worry if she couldn't find her.

As he turned back into Tethering Drove it began to rain. The drops were large, splatting against the tarmac, making the curled dead leaves of a beech hedge crackle, and landing on his uncovered hair like an ice-cold hand patting his head.

Chapter Twenty-Nine

Callum's sleep was fitful. He dreamed of Amber being hit by a car, heard the squeal of the tyres and woke suddenly, the noise still reverberating in his head.

He lay still for a moment, reorientating himself. It was still dark outside, and stars sprinkled the sky between grey clouds that were backlit by a ghostly moon. The sound of the accident was replaced by the pounding of blood rushing through his ears. He was hot and sweaty and tried to throw back the quilt to cool down. Something was stopping him. He snapped on the light. Amber was lying in the crook of his knees, curled into a relaxed ball.

Callum sat up abruptly, disturbing the cat. She blinked at him, yawned widely and stretched out a front leg towards his hand. Relief flooded through him and all his imagined scenarios melted away. He stroked her head, and she purred.

'Where have you been all night?' He released a long slow breath. She appeared to have the correct number of legs positioned in their intended locations. He ran a hand down her body and, instead of flinching from some injury, she rolled onto her back inviting him to tickle her tummy.

'All right. You keep your secrets.' He settled down and pulled the quilt back over his body. 'But when I get to work, I'll tell Daisy something she doesn't know about your satnav.'

Later, when he went upstairs to make himself some breakfast he saw the steak in the fridge. He felt a buzz of excitement that when he returned from work that evening, Rain would already be at home, probably embarked on some knitting project. He would cook her a special meal and ask her to move in with him.

* * *

Cookie gave a 'whoop' and grasped sheets of paper as they came out of the printer. He stood still and studied them. Callum watched from the fishbowl and when Cookie looked across in his direction, he beckoned him over.

Cookie shuffled the sheets of paper as he walked and was frowning when he stopped in front of Callum. 'I've got the birth certificates for Emilia and Felicity Garland, no problem.' He selected two sheets of paper and slid them across the desk towards Callum.

Callum examined them. 'Both registered locally. What about Charlotte and Darcie?'

'That's it, guv. I can't find anything for those names where the person is the right age. I did find a Charlotte in Aberdeen, but she's about eighty, so it's not her, is it?' He sounded downcast.

'Did you get the marriage certificate for George and Abigail?'

Cookie brightened up. 'Got that. Here it is. You were right, guv, Dunn was her maiden name.'

He slid another sheet of paper across the desk towards Callum who perused it in silence. Cookie fidgeted, his foot beating a tattoo on Callum's floor. He stood still when Callum lifted his head and gave him a hard look.

The marriage certificate showed that George Arnold Garland and Abigail Violet Dunn had married in St Giles Hermitage in Godshill in 2009. Callum had noticed the church alongside the road into Fordingbridge. It was a small building, brick-built with lattice windows, so the wedding must have been a small ceremony. He checked the birth certificates. 'Emilia was born in 2010 and Felicity in 2011. What does that tell us?'

'It means that Abigail already had the oldest two girls before she and George married.' Cookie grinned. 'Look at his initials. I bet I know what George's nickname was at school.'

'Concentrate on the girls, please, Cookie.'

'Yes, sorry, guv.' Cookie waggled his head from side to side and frowned. 'So that means, probably, that Charlotte and Darcie were born before they got married and…' He paused and flicked a finger against the side of his head. 'Ping! They probably aren't George's.' He looked at Callum and grinned.

'Good. That's a sensible assumption. Now have a look for births in 2007 and 2008 under their first names. We're pretty sure of the correct years as Charlie has just obtained her provisional driving licence and Darcie is younger by a year, according to the family. Try the surname of Dunn first, Abigail's maiden name, and then explore other names if you don't get a result.' Callum waited while Cookie made a note in his spidery handwriting on one of the pieces of paper before continuing, 'A probable place of birth is Birmingham.'

Brendan Stafford had lived and taught in Birmingham. He had relationships with local girls and many of them if his ex-wife was to be believed. Was that a stretch too far that he had children from one of these relationships? Callum thought not. Registering the births with Brendan's name as the father might have been problematic if he had thought he was keeping the relationships a secret from Victoria.

'Check under the surname Stafford, but that's a longshot,' Callum said. 'And see what you can find out about George Garland, please.'

He watched Cookie scoot back to his desk. They hadn't given any thought to George before now and they only had Abigail's assurance that he didn't know Brendan. Callum was not sure what the man did to earn a living, but whatever it was, it paid well enough to keep a wife and four daughters in horses in one of the most expensive areas of the country. How would George react if Brendan posed a threat to his happy family unit?

* * *

Daisy looked up from her desk. 'That's a disappointment,' she said.

'What is?' Bird wheeled his chair to one side to get an uninterrupted view of her.

'Actually, doubly disappointing.' Daisy walked to the fishbowl and Bird followed her.

Callum looked up. 'What's the problem?'

'No problem. I've been looking for Susie's Uncle Vinny. At worst, he was going to be a prolific burglar or Percy Snow and at best a mass murderer, but he hasn't read the script.' She perched onto the edge of Callum's desk and waved a piece of paper at him.

A puff of a printer-ink-laden air floated towards Callum. He stifled a smile. 'What is he then?'

'Besides being unaccommodating–' she paused when Bird laughed '–he really is her uncle. He's Janey's brother, and he's a writer.'

'Bad luck,' Bird said, and went back to his desk.

'He has come to our attention but for peaceful protests, sit-ins, that sort of thing. Hare Krishna and joss sticks. He is very keen on saving badgers and the environment. I don't think he's our killer, sir. Or our burglar for that matter, just a bit anti-establishment.' She huffed a breath upwards and floated some stray strands of hair out of her eyes.

'Is that all?' Callum asked.

She pulled a sad face and nodded, got off his desk and went back to her own.

* * *

Callum's desk phone rang, and the sergeant said he was putting through a call to him. He heard the connection click.

'DI MacLean,' he said.

'Hello. My name is Bethany. Are you the Callum that knows Rain Waters?' Her voice was calm and professional.

A cold stone of unease plummeted into Callum's stomach. 'I am. And you are?'

'I work with Rain. Now there's nothing to worry about, and Rain will be fine, but she was in a bit of an accident.'

A thousand questions barged into Callum's mind. What accident? Where was she? *HOW* was she? If Bethany said she would be fine, it meant that she wasn't fine right now.

'What happened?' He quelled the quiver in his voice.

'This morning we were walking across the road to the hospital car park together. She was sending a text and a car hit her.'

Callum took a sharp breath. Only a short while ago Rain had been telling him that they couldn't save another girl who had been hit by a car.

'She has bruises and scrapes,' Bethany continued, 'but nothing was broken.' She laughed. 'If you are going to get yourself run over, outside a hospital with a nurse next to you is a good place to be.'

Questions flooded into his mind, building up like water behind a closed lock gate.

'She asked me to get your mobile number,' Bethany said. 'She's planning on ringing you when she's ready for collection.'

Callum thanked her, replaced the receiver and sat back in his chair. He felt suddenly warm. The background noises from the office seemed muffled as if he was sitting in the bottom of a barrel. He tucked his long hair back behind his ears, closed his eyes and let out a long, slow breath. When he opened them, Daisy was standing on the other side of the desk.

'All right, Callum?'

Her frown and concerned voice made him wonder if she had been eavesdropping on his side of the conversation. He didn't like to share personal information, but if there was any possibility that it could impact on the team, then they deserved to know. He expected nothing less from them.

'I'm fine, Daisy, but Rain was hit by a car this morning when she finished her shift.'

He watched the myriad emotions chase across her face. 'Is she okay?' she asked.

'Apparently so. She's been checked over and I can collect her later.'

'That's good news. If you need anything, either of you, let me know.'

'What I need right now is to get these cases wrapped up as soon as possible.'

Chapter Thirty

Cookie bounced up from his chair, waved a hand at no one in particular and sat down again. 'I've found Charlotte and Darcie,' he said. 'I mean their birth certificates.'

Callum and Daisy walked over to his desk. 'Where?' Callum asked.

'Like you said, guv, Birmingham. Charlotte Lauren Dunn and Darcie Holly Dunn. Father unknown.'

'That doesn't mean that Brendan wasn't the father,' Daisy said.

'I think it's sensible to assume that he was,' Callum said. 'He traced them, probably by tracing Abigail first, and came here to find them. It explains the family connection that he spoke of and the reason he changed his will.'

'It also explains his weirdy comments on that video he took,' Cookie said.

Callum walked to the board on the back wall where the face of Brendan Stafford stared out at him. 'Okay, people.'

Chairs scraped and they moved towards the board.

His phone pinged a text and he opened it.

So you won't be too shocked.

He looked at the accompanying image. Rain stared back at him, a couple of Steri-Strips on her forehead, grazes across her cheek and nose, and puffy red areas of skin that promised to morph into colourful bruises. She was smiling into the camera.

He turned the phone around and showed the picture to the team.

'Poor Rain,' Daisy said and raised alarmed eyes to Callum.

'She looks as if she did ten rounds with Chantelle Reid and lost,' Cookie said, mock-punching the air.

'Ouch,' Bird said. 'But nothing broken, guv?'

'Rain tells me that it looks worse than it is. I'll believe that when I see it. Now update please. Cookie, how have you got on with George Garland?'

Cookie stood still. 'He's got his own company, and he works from home. He's a techie, into AI and got in on the ground floor when he started that company years ago. He's one of the top guys now. Mega bucks.' He loosened the knot on his *Finding Nemo* tie and slid a sideways look at Daisy. 'I don't get why he still lives here out in the sticks when he can afford to live in London, where it's all going on.' Cookie shook his head from side to side; eyebrows raised in disbelief.

'Because he's got better taste than that, more sense, and there's nowhere to ride in London that's anywhere near as good as the New Forest,' Daisy said, her cheeks turning pink.

Cookie shrugged. 'Just saying,' he said. 'Don't shoot the thought-carrier.' The look of wide-eyed innocence and the cheeky grin that Cookie shared with the rest of the team confirmed to Callum that the lad was baiting Daisy, who was a staunch supporter of living in the country.

'Cookie,' Callum growled.

At that very same moment, Bird prodded Cookie's shoulder with a non-too-gentle finger and Cookie laughed.

Daisy grinned. 'Okay, Cookie. You got me,' she said.

'Concentrate, Cookie. George Garland,' Callum said. 'Some of us want to get home tonight.' When the whole team speedily focused their attention on him, Callum registered the sharpness of his tone. His hand touched the phone in his pocket. Cookie was not responsible for Rain's injuries and the fact that the lad seemed unaffected by her plight was just Cookie being Cookie.

'Sorry, guv,' Cookie said without looking in the slightest bit remorseful. 'George started his first company when he left school, and he's always worked from home. Probably saved himself a shedload of money, doing that.'

'He lived at Crossways Farm with his mum before he got married,' Legs said. 'After the wedding they all lived there together. His mum, Winifred, died ten years ago. I haven't found a dad as yet.'

'Good. Keep looking,' Callum said. 'And dig deeper on George. Tomorrow we'll go and talk to George and Abigail. The girls should be at school during the day, so I'm hoping for expansive answers.'

'Aren't we going to arrest them now?' Cookie said.

'Nothing you have told me about them so far is illegal. Find me irrefutable evidence that they had contact with Brendan, that the communications were hostile, that they threatened him or he them, and then, yes, Cookie, we'll arrest George Garland. For now, what we have is mostly supposition. CPS won't prosecute on that.' Callum went into the fishbowl.

* * *

Callum's phone rang but he didn't recognise the number. 'DI MacLean,' he said, his voice gruff.

'So fierce,' Rain said against his ear.

'How are you?' He sat up in his chair.

'Almost fighting fit, and nothing that a few days' rest and a new phone won't put right. I borrowed Bethany's phone to call you.'

His heart seemed to be beating in his mouth. 'How are you really?'

'You'll see when you collect me later. Bit pissed off with the idiot who tried to run me over and annoyed that I have to buy a new phone. He ran over mine. Physically there is nothing wrong that a sticking plaster, arnica cream and a gallon of witch hazel won't put right.'

Callum listened to the purr of the cancelled connection against his ear and the relief that she was unharmed almost overwhelmed him.

* * *

Callum went out into the main office. 'Right, people. Let's have that update now. Cookie?'

Thay all gathered around Cookie's desk. Cookie shuffled his pieces of paper.

'I did the easy bits on George Garland first. Clean driving record and not on the PNC,' Cookie said.

Bird folded his arms. 'Just because he's not on the Police National Computer doesn't mean he's never committed a crime. It means he's never been caught committing one.'

'George is a big fish,' Cookie said. 'A rich big fish.'

'I'm always in the wrong bleedin' job,' Bird grumbled.

'He lets out the barns, but he uses the fields himself. Or rather the horses do.' Cookie looked up at them. 'Actually, if they are shorter than 14.2 hands high, they're ponies, not horses, and a hand measures–'

'Four inches,' Bird interrupted. 'Get on with it, Cookie.'

'Sorry, Bird.' Cookie's toe started to tap the floor. 'His mum died in 2014.'

'That's after he married Abigail,' Legs said. 'I couldn't find a Mr Garland senior.'

'I couldn't find one either,' Cookie said, 'or trace a death certificate for one. Winifred Garland never married, as far as I can see.'

'Does George have siblings?' Callum asked.

'No trace of any, guv,' Cookie said.

Callum thought that George could have been born out of wedlock, and there had never been a father figure in the household. It was not an unusual situation, and it didn't affect the investigation, but he found it useful to have background information on his suspects.

'Nothing suspicious that I could find,' Bird said from his perch on the desk. 'His social media shows him contacting people all over the world, at odd hours of the day, but nothing to raise an eyebrow at. I wouldn't want to pay his bleedin' phone bill though.'

'Thanks, Bird.' Callum turned to Legs. 'Anything on Abigail?'

'Same as George, squeaky clean in the DVLA and PNC departments,' Legs said. 'She runs the annual gymkhana, helps in an unofficial capacity at Breamore Primary School where all their girls used to go. They've moved up to senior school now. She helps with a local meals-on-wheels charity, The Riding for the Disabled, runs her B&B and looks after the girls' ponies and her horse.' She paused for breath.

'What does she do after lunch?' Daisy said, and Cookie laughed.

'All good background, but did you find any evidence of contact between either of them and Brendan Stafford?' Callum said.

They shook their heads. 'Absolutely nothing,' Daisy said.

'Right, people. First call of the morning we will go to Crossways Farm to speak to the Garlands and find out what they have to say in light of our discoveries.'

* * *

Daisy had suggested that a cottage pie might be easy for Rain to eat, and Callum had shopped on his way to the hospital to collect Rain. The steak meal he had planned would have to wait a day or two. He was glad he had taken Daisy's advice. Rain was dozing on the sofa, but the noise he was making with crockery and utensils woke her. He started spooning the steaming food onto plates.

'Hungry?' he called to her.

'I didn't get any breakfast or lunch,' she said, 'so yes.'

He added another dollop of food to her plate, put her fork back in the drawer and took out a spoon. He had offered to feed her, but one look at her face when he made the suggestion had him swiftly retract his offer. She did however ask him to find her next dose of painkillers.

When they had finished eating, he switched on the kettle to make a hot drink. Behind him he heard Amber come in through the cat flap. He was startled when Rain gave a short shriek followed by a surprised laugh. Callum swung round. Amber had jumped onto the sofa next to Rain and placed a lifeless mouse next to her.

'Sorry about that. I thought for a minute it was still alive,' Rain said with audible relief. She stroked the cat and Amber purred and pushed her head into Rain's hand. 'Thank you, Amber. That's very nice of you, but I have just eaten supper.'

Callum pulled off a sheet of kitchen paper. 'You're honoured. She's never brought me a mouse, dead or alive.' He picked up the creature in the paper, stroked the cat and went outside through the glass doors. He returned empty-handed. 'As you weren't hungry, I donated it to the local wildlife foodbank. Don't bring it back inside,' he added as Amber slipped out through the cat flap.

'Thanks, Cal. Do you mind bringing me my parcel and a pair of scissors? I want a quick peek at my wool while I drink my tea.'

'What are you going to knit?' he asked.

'You'll have to wait and see.'

Chapter Thirty-One

Callum awoke early. Rain was still sleeping beside him. She was pale but her breathing was rhythmic. When he touched her arm, it was warm. Already the cuts on her forehead looked less raw and her bruises were beginning to colour. The red blemish on her cheekbone was deepening to purple, the first tinges of indigo darkening the very centre. He stood and watched her sleep. He needed to be sure that she didn't have a fever and after a moment of hesitation, he gently placed his palm on her forehead.

She smiled. 'I'm awake,' she said, without moving her head or opening her eyes.

'I was just checking you were alive and kicking.' He withdrew his hand.

'Alive,' she said, 'not sure about the kicking bit.'

'No hurry for that.' He bent over her, kissed her gently on the lips and his long hair brushed her face.

She opened her eyes. 'That tickles, Cal.'

'No loss of sensation, that's good. Anything you need apart from painkillers before I go to work?'

'A cup of tea? And a new body if you've got one handy,' she joked. She began to sit up, gasped a sharp breath and completed the task more carefully.

Callum held his breath as he watched her struggle. He moved towards her, his hand outstretched.

'Don't even think about it. I can manage.' She grimaced. 'Use it or lose it is my philosophy. If I can't do something, I promise I'll ask you for help.'

'Good plan,' Callum said, stepping back. 'Tea coming right up. And, for the record, I like the body you've already got, no need to change it.'

'Lucky you because I wasn't planning to any time soon.' Rain smiled, the skin around her eyes bunching into soft folds. 'I'm not into plastic surgery.'

Callum huffed a short laugh. Amber, who was curled up on the bed, her body pressed against Rain's leg, lifted her head and squinted at him.

'And,' Rain said, 'will you just check there aren't any other little gifts from her on the bed or the floor? I don't think I'm quite up to running away from mice.'

When he returned, he placed her mug of tea on her bedside table and the strip of painkillers next to it.

'Not a mouse anywhere in sight,' he reported. 'I think we are going to be pretty busy today at work, so I might not get a chance to get home, but I will if I can. Do you want me to get Daisy to look in on you if I don't have time?'

'No thank you, Doctor,' she teased. 'I do not need a babysitter.'

'Fair enough.' He leaned down and kissed her. 'But promise me you'll ring if you need me.' He nodded at the landline phone on his bedside table.

'I promise,' she said. 'Now go to work and let Amber and I get our beauty sleep.'

Callum went back up the stairs to the kitchen two steps at a time.

* * *

'The girls should be at school,' Daisy said as she turned onto the driveway of Crossways Farm.

'I hope so,' Callum said. 'I think there are secrets in that family, things that George and Abigail have not shared with the girls and perhaps not with each other.'

'I think so too, but everybody has things they don't share with the world. It doesn't make them bad things.' Daisy drove slowly down the track beside the desiccated beech hedge. 'Jimmy told me that the pony he's found for Flissa is a 13.2 hh. New Forest gelding.'

'This is relevant because?' Callum asked as they pulled onto the cobbled yard and parked next to the camper van. The Defender and Fiat were there, parked next to one another, but the Jeep was missing.

'You said you wanted background information. Look, there's Abigail.' Daisy nodded towards the woman who was walking away from the house, accompanied by the two dogs. Her Puffa jacket was zipped up to the neck and two dog leads dangled from her gloved hand. She wore a brightly coloured tam-o'-shanter that Callum thought Rain would have liked.

They got out of the Navara, and the dogs raced across the cobbles to greet Daisy, their big-cat coats making them resemble large felines. Daisy fussed both the animals in turn and called across to Abigail who had stopped walking and was watching the detectives.

'Have you got a minute?' Daisy asked, straightening up and moving towards Abigail.

'I was just taking the dogs for a quick walk. The B&B guests are having a late breakfast because they're leaving today. The girls usually help with changeovers for extra pocket money, but they're at school. So I'm on my own.'

'We'll walk with you,' Callum said, fastening his jacket.

Abigail hesitated then nodded agreement.

In silence they walked down the track and past the barns. Penny's pickup was absent, and her barn was locked up. Keiron was somewhere in his building. Loud music echoed around the insides of the structure, and his vehicle was slewed across the open doorway.

Abigail's eyes were focused on the ground, and once or twice she shook her head from side to side as if dismissing her own suggestions. At the end of the track, their progress was halted by a padlocked five-bar gate. Abigail reached inside the top of her jacket and pulled out a key. It hung on a long loop of tape that enabled her to open the gate while still wearing it around her neck. She turned the key in the padlock and lifted the gate off its catch, holding it open so they could all pass through.

'That's a good idea, the long tape,' Daisy said. 'That means you can unlock the gate without having to get off your horse.'

'It's easier for the girls that way,' Abigail said, closing the gate behind them and securing the padlock. 'It was George's idea.'

As soon as they began walking along the track, Abigail said to Callum, 'You've come to ask me about Brendan, haven't you?'

'I have.' He tucked his hair back behind his ears and waited.

Chapter Thirty-Two

'I knew Brendan Stafford,' she said.

Their boots scrunched on the loose gravel beneath their feet, and Callum remained silent. Abigail glanced up at him once, then turned her eyes to follow her dogs as she began to speak. He wondered if she had consciously waited until she had left the family property before vocalising her thoughts.

'I met him when I was nearly sixteen. I had never met anyone like him before. He was clever and funny and beautiful. And I was young and impressionable and stupid.' She huffed a breath. 'God, I was so stupid.'

The track curved around the side of a hill, climbing as it went, exposing them to a cutting blast of chill wind as they headed north. It stirred the dead leaves from the beech trees that lined the track and lifted the smell of mouldering decay into the air.

'In my defence I was an only child, raised without a father but with a zealously protective mother, which I resented, so I turned our house into a war zone. I knew nothing about men, and I was flattered by his attention.' She swung the end of the dog leash at a pile of dead leaves, and they flicked up and danced away with the wind. 'We… celebrated my sixteenth birthday and nine months later

Charlie was born, followed eleven months after that by Darcie.' She shook her head slowly from side to side. 'I am embarrassed now at how naïve I was then. Our girls are much savvier. I thought he would divorce his wife and marry me.'

She walked in silence for a short distance along a single track that wound between twisted gorse bushes, and they silently followed her. When it widened out to a grassy slope, the detectives caught up and walked one on each side of her.

'After I had Charlie, my mother told me exactly what would happen and ordered me to stop seeing him. When I refused to do what she wanted, she threw me and Charlie out. Tough love, she called it.'

'Where did you go?' Callum asked, sensing that the solution did not involve Brendan Stafford.

'I had no idea what to do and I didn't realise at the time that I was already pregnant with Darcie. When I phoned Brendan and cried my tale of woe down the phone, he said goodbye, and good luck. With hindsight, that is exactly what I should have expected, and it was exactly what my mother said would happen.'

'What did you do? Go back home?' Daisy asked.

Abigail shook her head. 'That wasn't an option. There was a huge pub on that big roundabout on the ring road just up from where we lived. It was a bit rough, and they were always advertising for staff. I was lucky, they gave me a job, and I lived in one of their caravans out the back.'

'That must have been tough, with a baby to look after,' Callum said.

'You're not kidding,' Abigail said. 'I was at my wits' end when Darcie was born. I managed to contact Brendan once, but then he blocked me. He couldn't have made it plainer than that, could he?'

'How did you cope?' Daisy asked, tilting her head forward so she could see Abigail's face.

'Badly.'

Abigail called the dogs to her and clipped the leads onto their collars. Callum could hear the hum of tyres on tarmac and knew they were nearing the road.

'I was serving in the pub one evening and the babies were asleep in the caravan. George came in. I didn't know who he was, but he said he was at a conference up in Birmingham and didn't like staying in big hotels, so he was B&B-ing at the pub. We got talking. He was older than me – fifteen years older, in fact – but we hit it off.'

'He was not married?'

'No. Shy and single. He said afterwards it was love at first sight, for him.' She smiled at a memory. 'It took me a little longer to trust him, after Brendan.' The dogs trotted obediently beside her. 'George brought me down here to live, and we got married and then had Ems and Flissa. He adopted Charlie and Darcie, so we all have the same surname. He made us into a family. God knows where I'd have ended up without George. He saved me. And he is so close to the girls. Everything he does is for them. He was brought up without a father and family is very important to him.'

Callum wondered if her gratitude at being saved meant she would lie for him. He concluded that it would.

'His mum, Winn, was still alive then and lived in the house with us. She was so good with the girls. She died about ten years ago and the girls really missed her. My mum and I weren't on good terms, and she died not long after we got married so the girls never knew her. I know Charlie goes regularly to put flowers on Winn's grave and tell her everything that's happening. She was a nice lady.'

They walked along the verge on the opposite side of the road from the Drunken Donkey. The camper van belonging to the two lads had gone, and two wild ponies stood in the space it had vacated.

'Does George know about Brendan?' Callum asked.

Abigail shook her head. 'Only that there was someone and he abandoned us. I never told him who it was.'

'Do you think he found out?' Daisy asked.

'I don't think he has ever even thought about it. George is very, "if it's not broke don't fix it". He never bothers about things that don't affect him, or the family, especially not the things he can do nothing about. I can't see how he would have made a connection between me and Brendan.'

'But you recognised Brendan when he came to the village,' said Callum.

'He nearly gave me a heart attack. I saw him walking across the car park outside the shop,' Abigail said. 'He still drives a flashy car. I don't think he recognised me by sight. I looked a lot different twenty years ago, but he didn't look to have changed, except for having a bit less hair and bleaching it blond.'

'Did you speak to him?' Daisy asked.

'No. It was only that one time, and he was leaving as I was going in. That was the day before he died.'

'But you don't know why he was down here? Or what he wanted?'

'No. I don't know how he managed to trace us, but I don't think you have to be a member of Mensa to assume it has something to do with Charlie and Darcie.'

'Perhaps not,' Callum said. 'Where were you and George between four thirty and seven thirty on Friday evening? I have to ask.' They had a hall full of witnesses to their whereabouts for later that evening.

Abigail stopped walking. 'Not killing Brendan, that's for sure. I collected the girls off the bus from school, took them home, fed them and George and did the evening feeds for the horses. We left home about quarter to seven to walk to the hall because I had to open up and put out the chairs before the meeting.'

'Can anyone verify that?' Callum asked. 'Routine question,' he added when she frowned at him.

Abigail recommenced walking. 'The school bus driver saw me because I was parked waiting when he drew up. I gave a lift to a school friend of Charlie's who lives just down the road, and I dropped her at her gate. Her mum waved a thank you from their kitchen window.' Her face creased with concentration. She skirted an ice-fringed puddle. 'Then we saw Jimmy Eastwood about ten, or five to seven. He was just pulling into the village hall car park, and I asked him if he knew of a bigger pony for Flissa because she has really outgrown poor little Dumpling. Jimmy said he would put his thinking cap on. He has actually found one for her to try out.'

'And between those times?' Callum asked quickly before Daisy had an opportunity to comment on the newly found pony.

'Apart from family, five horses and two dogs, no one can vouch for me.' They followed her through the wicket gate that sided the cattle grid and walked down her driveway. The curled beech leaves whispered as they passed.

'No, wait,' Abigail said. 'Tom and Mickey came back just as we were leaving, and we passed them as they were parking up. That was a bit late for them. They're usually back earlier than that. I don't suppose you can spot birds in the dark.'

'And George?' Daisy asked.

'George was in his office when we got back from school. The girls all trooped in to say hello. Flissa had a drawing she wanted to show him, and Charlie had a computer question for him. They know it's no good asking me, I'm hopeless with technology but George is a genius.'

Abigail bent down and unclipped the dogs' leads as they came to the cobbled yard. 'They're still here,' she said, looking at the camper van.

'Was George in the house until you left to walk to the meeting?' Callum asked.

'He was. He nearly made us late actually. He had a Zoom, or whatever you call it, an online meeting with a man in South Africa and one from somewhere else. It dragged on a bit and Flissa went up to tell him we were going without him if he didn't hurry up.' She smiled. 'Flissa can twist him round her little finger. He was down the stairs double time, and they raced up the driveway, all five of them singing silly songs. I sometimes think I am the only sane person living in this house.'

Callum knew that George's actions would be easy to verify. It was looking less likely that the Garlands had anything to do with Brendan's death.

'And you had no contact of any sort with Brendan? No emails, no notes through the door, no texts or voicemails?'

Abigail shook her head. 'I promise, we had nothing to do with Brendan Stafford. I also think,' she said with a sigh, 'that it is time that I told George and the girls about Brendan.'

The black Jeep came slowly down the drive, turned onto the yard and pulled up next to the Defender. George got out, a folded newspaper under his arm, and walked across to stand next to his wife. The dogs cavorted at his feet, and he reached down a hand to stroke them. His hair was brushed back from his high forehead and his face looked so serious that Callum struggled to envisage him singing silly songs as he skipped up the driveway with the girls. But just because he couldn't visualise it didn't mean that it hadn't happened.

George nodded to Callum and looked at Abigail. 'Everything all right?' he asked.

'Fine,' Abigail said. 'They were just checking where we were before the gymkhana meeting when that man died.'

'I was here, working in my office' – he turned and pointed to an upstairs window of the house – 'and I had a conference call that ran over, and I nearly made us late for the meeting.'

'Thank you for the information,' Callum said, and heard Daisy's boots on the cobbles behind him.

'Well, if you don't need me.' George paused to look at Abigail. 'I'll be in my office.' He nodded to the detectives and walked towards the house, zapping locked his Jeep as he passed it. He dipped his head to acknowledge Tom Palmer who had just come out of the house towing a small, wheeled suitcase, his binoculars bouncing against the front of his jacket.

'Thanks for your time,' Callum said to Abigail.

'And good luck with the new pony. I hope it suits Flissa,' Daisy said over her shoulder as she and Callum walked back to her Navara.

Chapter Thirty-Three

Legs was on her feet as soon as Callum closed the outer office door.

'Guv, there were three more burglaries last night.' She followed him into the fishbowl.

'Tell me.' Callum sat in his chair.

'The first two were straightforward. Both the householders were at the parish council meeting, and it was the usual stuff that was taken. They got into one cottage through the back door, the key was under the mat, and the second through glass doors at the rear of the house.'

'And the third?' he asked, wondering why people still thought it was all right to keep an emergency key under the doormat when it was not rocket science to install a key safe.

'Not so straightforward. The victim was a Mrs Elsie Bridewell. She's an elderly widow, who lives alone and has mobility issues. Her cottage is down in the dip just past the ford in Godshill. She was at home when they came.'

'Go on.'

'We don't know much more than that, yet. When her carer arrived this morning, she found her lying on her sitting-room floor and her wheelchair was tipped over. Her carer took her to hospital to check that nothing was broken, which luckily it wasn't, so she'll be back home in about half an hour.'

Callum thought for a moment. 'I am going out. Give her details to Daisy and she, and I, will pay her a visit when I get back.'

'That'll give her time to get home and settled before you call on her,' Legs said, then walked across to Daisy's desk.

* * *

Frost had ridged the ruts in the grass verge outside Eddie Gilligan's cottage. Callum slowed to a stop, released his seat belt and zipped up his jacket before opening the driver's door and stepping down onto the crisp surface. Inside his garden, Eddie swung a long-handled axe into a block of wood and the crack, when it cleaved in two, carried like a rifle shot in the chill air. He was dressed in a T-shirt, jeans and work boots and Callum supposed that the evident exertion was saving Eddie from freezing to death.

The metal of the gate catch was so cold against Callum's fingers that it burned his flesh on the short contact. Eddie paused and turned towards his visitor, axe in one hand and a split log in the other. He tossed the log into a half-filled black gorilla tub.

Callum closed the gate behind him. 'I always think there's something cosy about an open fire, but they're a lot of work,' he said, then introduced himself.

'Miles said a policeman called to see me. Was that you?'

'It was. How are you now?'

Eddie reached his fleece from the top of a heap of cord wood and put it on. 'A bit anxious.' He pulled up the zip and thrust his hands into his pockets. 'Restless. I need to keep doing things.'

'Fancy a walk?' Callum looked towards the gate.

Eddie nodded and led the way out onto the narrow lane. Their boots left flattened depressions in the frost-stiff turf of the verge before they turned onto a footpath.

'Was it about that man that Irene ran over?' Eddie said.

Callum noted the use of her Christian name. 'It was, but he was already dead, so she didn't kill him.'

'That must be a relief. She's a nice lady.' Eddie hunched his shoulders then dipped his head to avoid a low branch.

'Is it okay if I ask you a couple of questions?' Callum ducked his taller frame beneath the overhanging bough, caught it with his head and the iced lace between the naked twigs shimmered.

Eddie slowed to walk beside Callum. 'It's fine. I made a promise to myself and others that I would always tell the truth, and I will.'

'I know,' Callum said. 'You have to be honest with yourself before you can be honest with others. And I very much appreciate that.'

Eddie turned his head, his eyes on Callum's face. 'What do you want to know, Inspector?'

'Tell me about deer poaching.'

Eddie's stride faltered but he quickly recovered. He filled his lungs then exhaled a cloud of vapour. 'Last Wednesday week, late afternoon, I shot a fallow buck up in Pitts Wood Inclosure. Do you want me to go on?' He glanced across to Callum before concentrating on the path ahead.

'Yes, please.'

'I punctured the chest then ran my blade up the neck. That severs all the major arteries, and the bleed out is very quick. I took off the head. Then the legs below the knee and hock. Is that what you wanted to know?'

'It is, thank you.' It confirmed what they already knew. 'What did you do with the carcass?'

Eddie hesitated. 'Look, I don't want to get anyone else into trouble. It was my problem.'

'What was, Eddie?'

'Lucy and my lack of money.'

'Lucy was your fiancée?' Callum said, keeping his tone conversational.

'*Was* being the operative word, and yes. I wanted to do the best by her, but I don't earn much and that was becoming a problem. I could feel her slipping away. I wanted to take her out somewhere special, get us back on track.' Bitterness crept into his voice. 'I was going to suggest a date for the wedding.' He huffed a noisy breath through his nose. 'That went well!'

The path curved round to the left and Callum realised they were probably going to rejoin the lane that would take them back to Eddie's cottage. 'How did you turn the meat into cash?'

When Eddie didn't respond, Callum stopped walking. Eddie walked on for a stride, then turned back to face him, shoulders hunched.

'This is just you and me chatting,' Callum said. 'It's not official. I'm just knotting off a loose end in my mind.' He walked forward and Eddie matched his stride.

'I took it to Harry Kingman. I don't have a Gamekeepers' ID card, so I don't have any tags. You know, the official ones,' Eddie said. 'Harry offered me a pittance even though it was a clean carcass. He took the venison into his cold store and told Irene to take the money out of the till to pay me.' He glanced at Callum. 'Irene gave me extra money. I don't want to get her into trouble.'

'Like I said, this is off the record.' Callum didn't ask who owned the gun he had borrowed because he was sure that Eddie would tell him.

The undergrowth to the side of the track rustled and they paused. A cock pheasant ran out squawking a noisy protest then took off and whirred away, its lengthy feathers trailing like a kite tail.

'She threw the ring back at me and called me a loser.' Eddie lowered his head. 'I didn't cope very well.'

'Not something that's easy to cope with, I imagine,' Callum said.

Callum heard the growl of an engine and knew they must be approaching the lane. They avoided a trailing bramble, strode across a shallow ditch filled with ice-edged water and stepped onto the tarmac lane.

'Can I ask you something?' Eddie said.

Callum could see his vehicle parked ahead. It felt churlish to refuse after Eddie had been so forthright and honest.

'Try me.' Callum slowed and stamped the wet leaves from the soles of his boots.

'Miles said you know about *The Steps*. How?'

Callum's instinct was to deflect the question, but a truthful answer could not harm anyone now. 'Not for myself. My best friend at school, Malcolm, was faced with a situation that he didn't know how to cope with, and he said drink made him forget.'

Eddie nodded his understanding and slowed as they reached Callum's car. 'How is he doing now?'

'Not as well as you are.' Callum folded his arms across his chest and leaned against the cold bonnet. The colour had leached from the sky and three dark *V* shapes dropped down and landed on the naked branches of a beech tree. 'His funeral was the day after our final exams.' The cold air made his eyes sting, so he closed them for a moment. When he opened them again Eddie was studying him.

Eddie's voice took on a positive tone. 'That's not going to happen to me, Inspector.'

'I'm pleased to hear it.' Callum levered himself upright and took his keys out of his pocket.

'Inspector, what's going to happen about what I told you? I know I was in the wrong.' A frown puckered his brow, and he seemed to be holding his breath.

Callum smiled. 'Nothing. It was all off the record. Least said…'

‘Soonest mended. My gran used to say that.’ Eddie blew out a long breath and the tightness eased out of his shoulders. ‘Thank you, Inspector. I won’t be doing it again.’

Taking no further action was the best result for Eddie, but it rankled that shelving the matter meant taking no action regarding Harry. For now.

Callum glanced in his door mirror as he pulled away from the side of the road. Eddie raised a hand in farewell and turned towards his gate. They had both made small gestures, but ones that neither man would forget.

Chapter Thirty-Four

Elsie Bridewell lived in a bungalow that was dwarfed by the houses on either side of her. Her roof was iced with frost and for some reason made Callum think of Hansel and Gretel. A pine tree stood behind the bungalow, flanked by the winter skeletons of silver birch trees. A thick laurel hedge surrounded the entire plot, breached only by a cattle grid guarding the entrance. Daisy's tyres rattled across it and Callum saw that another vehicle was already parked at the front of the property. Daisy drew up alongside it. She looked through the side windows of the other vehicle as she brushed past it to get to the rear of her Navara.

'Carer, I expect,' she said as they walked to the front of the property.

Through the stained-glass panel in the top of the door, Callum saw a figure walking through the hall towards them.

'You're probably correct,' he said.

The carer ushered them into a sitting room where classical music was playing. A log burner set in the brick fireplace was filling the room with a cosy warmth and Callum unzipped his jacket. A woman propelled her wheelchair across the floor towards them.

'I keep it warm because I can't dance a jig anymore. I'm Elsie Bridewell. How may I help?'

Elsie had a thin, but upright torso. She had short grey hair above a gaunt bony face and wore a double string of pearls around her neck. Her powder-blue twinset was a fine knit and did nothing to hide her prominent collar bones. Her legs were concealed beneath a red-and-green tartan rug and Callum experienced a moment of panic at what could have happened to Rain.

Callum introduced himself and Daisy. 'How are you, Mrs Bridewell?'

'Absolutely bloody livid,' she said, and Daisy laughed. 'I wouldn't have answered the door if they had knocked, but they let themselves in through the French windows.' She turned her eyes briefly towards the light source. 'I hadn't got around to locking up yet – more fool me,' she said. 'Do sit.' She pointed to a tan corduroy sofa.

'Did they hurt you?' Callum asked, seating himself next to Daisy.

'Only my pride. They pushed me out of my chair, and I fell onto the carpet, so it was a soft landing. But, of course, I couldn't get up, so I had to lay there and watch them take my late husband's Rolex watch that was engraved and given to him by the late Lord Mountbatten just before he was assassinated, and all of his medals.'

'Did they threaten you?' Daisy asked.

'Verbally, but I didn't take any notice of their nonsense.'

'Did you recognise them?' Daisy said.

'Balaclavas, my dear. Black knitted sort. But I'm fairly certain that the men were white, medium height, one of the two was slightly portly and had a limp and they both spoke with a London accent. They wore gloves, as one might expect.'

Daisy was making notes. 'Any idea of age?' she asked.

'Mine or theirs?' Elsie laughed. 'I'm ninety-two and I should estimate that I gave them a good twenty years, my dear.'

Callum pointed to the call alert button hanging from a cord around Elsie's neck. 'Were you not wearing that last night?' he asked.

'I have already been sufficiently chastised by my carer and then by the nurses at the hospital. No, I wasn't. I was quite comfortable laying on the floor listening to music. I didn't expect them to come back, and I was correct because they didn't.'

'We might have had a better chance of catching them if you had been able to alert us immediately,' Daisy said gently. 'And you wouldn't have had to be here on your own all night.'

'Granted,' Elsie said. 'But I am never on my own.' She wheeled across the carpet and lifted a silver-framed photograph from a shelf. 'Bertie,' she said and wiped her forearm across the glass before turning it to show Daisy an attractive man in full dress uniform with a twinkle in his eyes. 'We talked nearly all night. He was always great company.' She lowered the frame onto the tartan rug that covered her lap. 'My great-grandsons were going to get his medals. They are both in his old squadron. That is what I find so very disappointing.'

'We'll leave you in peace now but if you think of anything else, please let us know,' Callum said, rising to his feet.

'The portly one did a lot of grumbling about his legs aching. No stamina, these youngsters.'

Callum saw Daisy smother a smile.

'When they left,' Elsie continued, 'they were driving a diesel vehicle, not one of those creepy electric ones, and they parked outside in the lane because it didn't rumble over my cattle grid.'

'That's very helpful,' Callum said. 'We'll let ourselves out.'

Daisy's Navara rumbled over the cattle grid, and she stopped before driving out onto the road, idling the engine.

'Are you thinking what I'm thinking, Callum?'

'Which is?' He glanced left and right and motioned her to drive on.

She eased the car into gear and pulled away. 'Which is, that it's too much of a coincidence for the burglars to be anyone other than the Palmers. Don't you think?' she added when he didn't immediately reply.

'It's a fair assumption.' Elsie's comments had already cemented it for him.

'Elsie said there were two of them, one had a limp and was a complainer, they had London accents, and they drive a diesel motor. What else do you need?' Her voice was a note higher than usual, and she flicked an impatient look at him.

'I'm not disagreeing with you.'

Daisy let out a noisy breath. 'But?'

'But nothing. Now we get proof.'

* * *

Daisy went across the outer office and stood beside Bird's desk. Their heads were close together as they bent forward to read some information on Bird's screen. They both turned and looked towards the fishbowl, an unasked question in the tilt of their heads. Callum nodded for them to come over.

Daisy sat on the chair and Bird leaned against the door jamb.

'It's been bugging me, guv, that Percy Snow's prints were on the back of Harry Kingman's pickup, especially as Harry says he's never driven it to London,' Bird said. 'So, I did a bit of digging on the Reindeer Gang.'

'I'd never heard of them before,' Daisy said, 'but this might be relevant, sir.'

'Go on,' Callum looked at Bird. 'What did you find?'

Bird took a pace inside the fishbowl. 'The Reindeer Gang operated in the East End of London in the eighties. There were seven of them, all brothers with the surname Snow.'

'Where did "Reindeer" come from then?' Daisy asked.

'Old Ma Snow was a moneylender, and her old man got shot doing a bank job, so she had to up her game because she had seven growing lads to feed. She got them all working for her collecting dues, running a protection scam with the odd bit of thieving thrown in for a bit of variety. Her boys were Davy and Donny, Peter and Victor, and Charlie and Percy and Ray. Same first letters as Santa's reindeers.'

'Donner and Blitzen, and Prancer and Dancer. I can't remember the rest,' Daisy said. 'That makes sense.'

Callum thought he remembered there being nine reindeer, but it wasn't relevant just now.

'And the Met boys nicknamed them the Reindeers,' Callum said, 'because their surname was Snow?'

'Spot on, guv. And they did a lot of damage for a good while. They had a reputation for being brutal and on the rare occasions they got arrested, nobody wanted to testify against them.'

'Same old,' Daisy said. 'I bet their brief made a mint.'

'Probably,' Bird said. 'It all went tits-up, though. When they planned their last job, which was a big one, the boys in blue got tipped off and were waiting for them mob-handed. The gang tried to do a runner and crashed into a bridge in the pursuit. A couple of them were killed and the rest were injured to some lesser or greater degree. The worst damage was to Prancer aka Percy. The Met reckoned his antenna didn't pick up all the channels, if you know what I mean.'

'I don't; what do you mean?' Cookie frowned at Bird before turning away to answer his phone.

'That he's not playing with a full deck,' Bird said. 'He wasn't wearing a seat belt and went through the windscreen. He broke his pelvis, both legs and an arm, and his face was a bit of a mess. He got the lightest sentence cos they weren't sure he really understood what he was doing. He just did what he was told. It looks like Percy and Donny are the only two left alive now. The old lady's dead, and most of the others died in jail.'

'So, Harry didn't go to London,' Daisy said, 'Percy Snow came to Fordingbridge.'

'That's about the size of it, guv. They've retired and taken up birdwatching in their old age.'

'I can think of warmer hobbies,' Daisy said, yet again. 'But if the Palmers are the Snows, and it looks like they are, then we know how that print got on Harry's Ranger, and it was nothing to do with Harry.'

'Because he parks on the pavement in everybody's way, so they probably just touched it as they passed by,' Bird said.

'Good work,' Callum said. 'That's enough for us to bring them in.'

'You don't reckon they're planning on starting a protection racket down here do you, guv?' Bird said with a grin.

'Wait, guv,' Cookie called across the office to Callum, waving his arm in the air and replacing his phone receiver. 'There's something else.'

'Well? Hurry it up. Abigail said the Palmers are checking out this morning and we need to get there before they go.'

'A chap sent us some dashcam footage,' Cookie said. 'He's got one of those flashy infrared night-vision cams. I've just checked it, and the footage is clear as a bell. He was driving over Breamore Marsh towards Woodgreen Wednesday evening. There was a camper van parked half on, half off the verge so he slowed down to pass it. Said he didn't want to end up in the ditch in the dark. It was outside Rush Cottage and two figures were coming out of the gate.'

'Relevance?' Callum said sharply.

'This morning,' Bird said, 'the owners of Rush Cottage phoned to report a burglary.'

'When? Last night?' Callum said.

'They're not sure when, guv. They were away from Wednesday afternoon at a family celebration, sixtieth wedding anniversary in Devon. They drove back this morning.'

'That's diamond,' Cookie said. 'Diamonds. Get it?' He laughed.

Bird ignored him. 'It was the usual stuff that was taken. They remember having a conversation with a couple of birdwatchers when they were loading suitcases into their motor on Wednesday. I reckon the pair were the Palmer brothers.'

'Evidence?' Callum asked.

'The dashcam footage,' Cookie said. 'It shows two men leaving the property later that evening. It also clearly shows the VRN of the vehicle parked outside and partially obstructing the carriageway.'

'And the vehicle registration number belongs to?' Daisy asked.

'Donald James Snow. Not even false plates. Dumb or what?' Cookie swivelled round in his chair and shouted, 'Yee-ha.'

'Now I feel such a fool, sir,' Daisy said. 'I believed what Tom told me when you were talking to Penny.'

'Which was?' Callum said.'

'That they were looking for sanderling and red kites on Breamore Marsh,' Daisy said. 'He didn't say anything about jewellery and cash.' She shrugged into her jacket.

'They were telling you porkies,' Bird said. 'The sanderling is a migrant, but it's a coastal bird so they're not going to see one here.'

'Perhaps they didn't know that?' Callum said.

'That's possible,' Bird said. 'But red kites? There are hundreds of the bleedin' things. They live here all year, and there's so many of them now that I reckon they are driving out the buzzards. If Tom thinks they are winter visitors, he's talking out of the back of his head.'

Callum had seen the raptors himself, soaring on the summer thermals, their distinctive forked tail making them easy to differentiate from the wedge-tailed buzzards against the light background of the sky.

'He was either telling you a load of old cobblers on purpose, Deedee,' Bird said, 'or he doesn't know what he's talking about.'

'The Palmers looked the part.'

Callum detected a tinge of defensiveness in her tone.

Daisy patted her pockets presumably to locate her keys. 'Tom still had his binoculars round his neck when he was loading the van to leave.'

'Still playing the part. Let's get over there,' Callum moved swiftly towards the door. 'Come on, everybody. Quick as you can.'

'Wilco, guv.' Bird grabbed his jacket from the back of his chair.

Daisy was on Callum's heels as they raced out into the corridor. 'I said they were idiots to be birdwatching in this weather,' she said.

Chapter Thirty-Five

Daisy raced out of Fordingbridge and along the road to Godshill. She turned into Crossways Farm, drove quietly down the track and both detectives unfastened their seat belts on the move. As she was about to turn into the cobbled yard, the camper van pulled onto the track in front of them and the vehicles stopped bonnet to bonnet. Donny looked through the windscreens straight at Callum.

'Donny's mine,' Callum said and slid out of the passenger door. He strode to the other vehicle and yanked open the driver's door before Donny had time to unfasten his seat belt.

Daisy opened the passenger door. 'Would you step out of your vehicle please, Mr Palmer.' Her tone of voice made it clear to Percy that it was an order, not a question.

Percy looked angrily at his brother. 'I told you this would happen, you greedy bugger.'

'Shut it,' Donny said in a quiet measured voice. 'I'm warning you.'

'And I'm warning you,' Callum said as he heard Daisy issuing a caution to Percy. 'No heroics, Mr Snow.' At the first mention of his real name, Donny tensed his muscles. 'Get out now.' Callum's words were curt. 'Face away from me and place your hands against the side of your vehicle, legs wide apart. Now.'

Donny slowly got out of the driver's seat. Callum reached for his handcuffs and snapped one bracelet closed around Donny's right wrist. Donny pulled his arm away sharply and started to shift his weight to bring his legs together. Callum held fast to the tethered arm and forcefully kicked the ankle of one of Donny's splayed legs. Donny folded into a heap on the gravel like an uncooperative deck chair and Callum reached down and snapped the other cuff closed behind the man's back.

'Aagh. You've hurt my knee,' Donny shouted.

'Tough,' Callum said quietly. He looked through the open doors of the cab to Daisy. 'Okay?' he asked.

'Cuffed, guv,' she confirmed.

Callum heard the wail of the two-tones and saw flashing blue lights reflected on the windows of Daisy's Navara. Doors slammed and Bird was at his side. Legs went to join Daisy, where she dwarfed the cuffed Percy.

'All sorted, guv. Wagon's on the way.' Bird reached down to grasp one of Donny's arms as Callum took hold of the other and they lifted him to his feet. They steered him around the rear of his vehicle to join his brother who stood compliantly next to Daisy.

'I told you this would happen.' Percy spat out his words. 'I told you, didn't I? But would you listen? You always have to know best.' He tried to remonstrate with his arms, but Legs retained a firm hold of the cuffs.

'Shut it,' Donny said quietly. 'Say nothing.'

'It's too late. I should never have listened to you.' Percy tried to free his arms from Legs' hold. He was red in the face and in struggling, nearly fell over.

'Steady,' Legs said, 'take it easy or you're going to hurt yourself.'

When both men had been cautioned, Donny stayed quiet but sent threatening looks towards his brother. Percy wasn't intimidated now that he had a protective circle of police officers around him, and there was a lot that he wanted to get off his chest. No amount of shushing from Donny was going to stop him from speaking his mind.

'It was his idea, us pretending to be birdwatchers so we could case the joints,' Percy said. 'Bloody brilliant idea that turned out to be.'

'What did you do with the items you stole?' Callum asked.

'Back of the van,' Percy said straight away.

Donny swung a boot at his brother but missed and hit the side of his own vehicle. Bird moved Donny further away and backed him up against the beech hedge as Callum slid open the side door of the camper van. Callum climbed inside, dipping his head to avoid hitting it and Daisy followed him. She had no trouble in walking upright and moving to the back, opened the rear door to let in more light. Both sides of the vehicle were kitted out with drawers that ran from floor to ceiling. There was no evidence of any equipment that camper vans were usually fitted with, like sinks or hobs.

'Ooh, look,' she said, pulling out one of the drawers. 'I think I've found Ruby Dixon's good pearls.' She slipped on clear gloves and pulled the drawer open fully to peer inside. 'Looks like the rings she described as well.' She lifted out some of the contents. 'And I think this ring was on the inventory from the burglary along Hale Purlieu. The one when the golf trophy was taken.' She held up a distinctive diamond ring for Callum to see before putting it back where she found it.

Daisy pulled open another drawer and gave a cursory glance at the contents. 'There's so much stuff here, sir, I don't think we're the only villages they hit. This is going to take a bit of sorting out.'

Callum pulled open a couple of drawers on the opposite side of the van. She was right. There were hundreds of pieces of jewellery all stowed in plastic containers within the drawers. The nearest collection was made up of heavy gold chains, an identity bracelet and a selection of sparkling rings. He hoped the bracelet was engraved; it would make tracing the rightful owner easier. He turned his head sideways to read the scrap of paper in amongst the valuables.

'That's very helpful of them,' he said to Daisy. 'They've put labels in each container, so they know where they stole it from.'

'Minimises the chance of offering it for sale in the area they nicked it from where someone might recognise it.'

Out of the corner of his eye, through the open rear door, Callum saw that George and Abigail stood on the cobbles watching events unfold. He held up a flat hand to warn them not to come any closer. George nodded his understanding and looped his arm across Abigail's shoulders, pulling her body close to his. Then they both turned and looked down the track towards the barns as Keiron's pickup growled into view and skidded to a halt when he saw that the road ahead was blocked.

Callum glanced cursorily into a couple more drawers that all seemed to contain the spoils of the burglaries. In the third drawer, he found the trophy watch, still in its presentation box of red leather, a Rolex and an impressive collection of military medals. Daisy was right. This was a much larger stash than just those goods stolen in the burglaries on their patch. He slid open a drawer near the rear of the vehicle and took in a sharp breath.

'What, sir?' Daisy moved to stand beside him. The emerald ring she was holding reflected green shards against her face, giving her the look of a sickly ghost. She looked in the drawer that Callum held open and sucked in a breath. 'Wow.' She put the ring back where she had found it and gave her attention to Callum's finds. 'Knuckledusters,' she said. 'They look pretty gruesome. I wouldn't fancy being punched by them.'

The two items were side by side in the small drawer. One was a four-ring brass affair, very plain and sturdy. The second one was more elaborate. The metal was brighter, and a dragon entwined itself around the finger holes, the raised spines of its tail producing a lethal hitting edge. Callum heard Keiron get out of his pickup and ask George what was going on. He didn't catch George's reply.

'Nasty,' Daisy said, lifting the weapon in her gloved hand. She turned it to the natural light coming through the rear door. 'That's got traces of blood on it, and stuck to those spines, that looks like fabric.' She replaced it carefully in the drawer. 'We need SOCOs here.'

'Martha said if we found her the knuckleduster then she would be able to match it to the injuries on Brendan's body.' Callum stepped back swiftly as Daisy pulled open the lowest drawer, narrowly missing his shins.

'Look, sir.' She reached in and took out a knife. 'Probable murder weapon?' Daisy held it up for him to see more clearly.

'Unlikely. It looks clean to the naked eye, and we're still waiting for Martha's say-so on the weapon, but I don't think this blade fits the profile,' he said, taking the knife and moving to the open doorway to examine it in a better light.

Gravel scattered as Keiron moved towards the van. 'That's my knife, the one that was nicked,' he shouted. He reached out a hand.

'Stay back.' Daisy took the knife from Callum and bagged it.

Callum climbed down the rear steps onto the gravel. He stood in front of Keiron, bringing the thatcher's progress to a halt. 'What makes you think it's your knife?'

'I know my own knife. If you don't believe me, look at the handle. It'll have "KT" carved into it on the underside. Go on, look.' Keiron pointed towards Daisy who stood on the rear step of the van.

Callum kept his eyes on Keiron as Daisy put the bag in his outstretched hand.

'Here, sir.'

He examined the handle then tilted the bag towards Daisy so that she could see that "KT" was clearly etched into the handle. He returned the knife to Daisy.

'I told you it was mine. Give it here.' Keiron again stretched out his arm towards the detectives.

'It's evidence. We will be keeping it for now,' Daisy said, retreating into the van.

'Stay there,' Callum ordered and walked round to the side of the camper van, leaving a red-faced Keiron in the centre of the track.

The Garlands remained standing side by side on the cobbled yard and both of their dogs now stood next to them.

Bird had steered Donny onto the verge that edged the track and was maintaining a firm grip on the handcuffs. Callum assumed that because his officers had separated the brothers, Donny was still being obstructive. Legs no longer held onto Percy's restraints and had let him sit down on the step beneath the van's side door. She had moved the cuffs around to the front of his body, presumably to aid his ability to balance. Percy looked physically uncomfortable and angry, his red face making the scar down the side of his cheek stand out like a relief map of the coastline of Chile.

'That bloke,' Percy said, looking up at Callum. 'It was his own fault he got hurt. He should have kept his nose out, like he was told.'

Donny tried to pull away from Bird and lunge at Percy, but Bird twisted the cuffs and Donny yelled out in pain.

'No, you don't, fella.' Bird jerked the cuffed hands high in the air with one hand and pressed down on the back of Donny's head with the other until the suspect was nearly bent double. It was inelegant but effective and Bird steered Donny up the track, away from the scene. 'The wagon's here, guv. I'll put him away, shall I?'

'Good move,' Callum said. Percy would be more forthcoming if his younger brother was out of earshot.

Callum turned his attention to Percy. Behind him gravel rattled beneath the detective's boots, and Donny cursed at Bird.

Callum squatted down in front of the seated Percy, his forearms resting across his thighs. 'How did the man get hurt, Percy?'

'He was nosing round the van. I was inside, putting stuff in the drawers like I always do when we get back because that's my job, see. I didn't know he was there. I opened the back doors so I could get a bit of extra light from the yard lights to see what I was doing. It was dark outside, see, and the Garlands had just all gone to some meeting, so I thought we was on our own.' Percy inclined his body towards the rear of the van and pointed at Keiron with his cuffed hands. 'But that's where he was, stood right there, see, with his phone in his hand, looking at the jewels I had in my hands.'

'That must have been a surprise,' Callum said.

'Surprise?' Percy swivelled back to face Callum. 'Too bloody right, it was. I shouted at him, and he started to run away down the track.' He nodded his head in the direction of the barns. 'I'm not too hot on me pins, but our Donny was in the front of the van and was after him like a greyhound out of trap 3. I followed, a bit slower, like. Don must have had the dusters in his pocket, cos when I got down there, he was giving the bloke a right pasting. I told him, "Don, that'll do," but he kept going, didn't take no notice of me at all.'

Bird came forward and stood next to Callum. 'You didn't hit him?' he asked.

'Do I look like I can fight, guv'nor?' Percy said with a shake of his head. 'No, I never hit him. I just wanted to give him a fright and nick his mobile in case he'd took pictures.'

'Did you ask him for his phone?' Bird said.

'Didn't have to. He offered his phone to Don but Don knocked it out of his hand. I reckon the bloke thought it'd stop Don hitting him.'

'And did it?' Daisy asked, coming round from the back of the van.

'Nah. He hit him again, right in the breadbasket, and the bloke went down. He might have been all right if he'd stayed there. I picked up his phone and the stupid bugger started getting to his feet and shouting about going to see you lot. His car keys fell out of his pocket, and he tried to pick them up, but Don got to them first.'

'What did he do with them?' Callum asked.

'Chucked them. They hit the side of the barn and went down in all that straw. Dunno where exactly, it was dark.'

'How did he come to get stabbed?' Daisy asked.

'He wasn't stabbed. He was runover, wasn't he?' Percy's eyes flicked uneasily from Daisy to Callum.

'Tell us what happened after Donny threw away the keys,' Callum said.

'I saw Don pick up something near the straw when he was throwing away the keys. The bloke was staggering away up the track clutching his guts and Don pulled his jacket up over his head and punched him in the back once more. Maximum effect. The bloke went down again, and I knew he'd landed a kidney punch. That's one of his specialities, kidneys. He's an animal.'

'And you left him there?' Callum said.

'Yes, he was breathing and groaning so I figured he was okay.'

'But you must have heard that he died?' Daisy said.

'Yeah, course we did, but not till the next day and they said he was run over. I said we should move on there and then, PDQ like, but Donny said it would look suspicious so we should stay for a bit longer and carry on as normal.' He shifted his position to ease his leg. 'I've had enough of it, see. I wanted to stop. But stopping Donny when he's got the bit between his teeth is like trying to stop a frigging loco.' He was silent for a moment, seeming to consider his next words. 'Here, how did you know it was us?' Percy struggled to his feet and Callum supported his elbow until he had gained his balance. 'Donny said it was foolproof, going off with the bins round our necks every morning, scoping the joints when we was pretending to be birdwatching. He said no one would clock us. Arrogant tosser.'

Callum looked at the others as he spoke. 'Let's just say, a little bird told me.'

Legs and Daisy laughed.

Chapter Thirty-Six

The team had loaded both the brothers into vehicles when Callum received a text from Martha.

Murder weapon is a thatcher's reeding pin.

She had added a shocked emoji face.

Callum passed his phone to Daisy with the text still open. Keiron stood next to his pickup, arms folded, leaning against the bonnet, waiting. He could not leave the scene until they had removed the vehicles blocking the track. Callum strode towards Keiron who had watched the Palmers be arrested. Daisy was a stride behind when Callum reached for Keiron's wrist and twisted it up behind his back.

'Keiron Tapper, I'm arresting you–' He reached his hand behind him for his cuffs and realised that Donny was wearing them. 'Bird. Cuffs,' Callum called over his shoulder. 'I'm arresting you for the murder of Brendan Stafford.' His caution was interrupted by Keiron ripping his wrist out of Callum's grasp before sprinting past his pickup, heading towards the barns.

Bird shouted 'shit' and raced to join Callum who was in pursuit of Keiron. Daisy flashed past the male officers, arms pumping, and launched herself at the fleeing figure.

Her arms wrapped around his hips and they both crashed onto the gravel. There was a moment of silence broken by rooks cawing in the nearby silver birch trees. They lifted off and flapped away like black rags. Abigail shrieked a breath. Keiron had landed with Daisy on his back, one arm trapped beneath him. With the other, he punched awkward blows upwards onto Daisy's back.

Callum reached her first. 'Okay?' he asked her, grasping Keiron's pummelling fist.

'I will be as soon as I get my arms back.'

'Holy shit,' Bird said catching up and dragging Keiron's other hand out from beneath his body and cuffing it. 'Nice try, fella.'

Daisy untangled her arms from Keiron's body, stood up and brushed gravel from her jacket. 'That's better.' She tucked a few stray hair strands back from her face. As the men fastened the handcuffs on their prisoner and completed the previously interrupted caution, she began patting her pockets.

Bird marched a smug-looking Keiron past his parked pickup and towards the police vehicles.

'What are you looking for?' Callum asked Daisy.

'Your phone. I was just going to return it to you when you jogged past me,' she said.

'There can only be one Usain Bolt,' he said, noting that she was moving freely and appeared uninjured by her flying tackle.

Daisy withdrew his phone from her pocket and looked at it. 'Oh dear. Sorry, sir.'

'It can't be helped. As long as you are all right.' He reached out his hand for his phone. Hopefully it was just a smashed screen.

'I'm fighting fit, thanks. And your phone's fine, too. I was only joking,' she said, passing the mobile to him.

Callum huffed a breath, slipped his phone back into his pocket and followed Daisy up the track where she had stopped to speak to the Garlands. The dogs looked up at her, tails wagging, and she patted each in turn.

'Sorry about blocking your access. The tow truck is on the way to recover the camper van, so it won't be for too long.'

George frowned down at Daisy. 'Are you sure you're okay? That was quite a tackle.'

'Perfectly fine, thanks,' she said as Callum joined her. Daisy leaned towards the Garlands and stage-whispered, 'But don't tell the boss I'm uninjured. If I'm lucky I might get a couple of days off.'

'You should be so lucky,' Callum said quietly as he walked behind her to their vehicle.

* * *

They entered the office to an accompanying 'whoop-whoop' from Cookie. Right hand held high, he whirled an imaginary lariat around his head. Callum stopped walking. He took his phone from his pocket and reread the text message from Martha.

Murder weapon is a thatcher's reeding pin.

Below the emoji, she had added "Perp LH".

Callum looked around the room for Daisy and she reversed through the outer door carrying a tray of drinks.

'Fortification before the interviews,' she said, resting the tray on the corner of Bird's desk and passing him a mug.

Callum took the coffee she passed to him. 'Is Keiron right- or left-handed?' he asked the room.

Activity paused as they all thought about the question.

'Right,' Daisy said, moving her tray to Cookie's desk.

'I reckon you're right,' Bird said. 'He's right-handed. Why?'

Callum told them about Martha's text.

'I only read as far as the face,' Daisy said. 'You were already on the move, so I put your phone in my pocket and joined the pursuit.'

'Bollocks,' Bird said. 'No wonder he was smirking about his alibi when we brought him in.'

'Flying tackle for nothing,' Daisy said, turning away to answer her phone.

Callum had run various scenarios through his head on the way back to the station. A reeding pin was an easy-to-lay-hands-on weapon for a thatcher. What he did not find so easy to determine was a motive. If Keiron could prove he was elsewhere on the evening Brendan was murdered, there would be no need to worry about his motive.

'Bird, Cookie, check out his alibi, please.'

'Wilco, guv.' Bird put down his mug and picked up his phone.

In the fishbowl, Callum rang Martha.

She answered on the second ring. 'MacLean. You got my text then. Written backup will be with you later and I do hope you are not ringing to question my findings.' She was moving papers and the sibilant whispering of them made him think of birds' wings fluttering in his fir tree.

'Absolutely not, Martha.' He paused to couch his next question in a diplomatic way. 'It took a long time to find a murder weapon?'

The papers stopped moving and Martha made a noise in her throat. 'It won't surprise you to know that more people get shot, stabbed with a knife, bashed over the head or get hit by a car than get stabbed with a reeding pin. It's a minority sport, MacLean. Fewer examples to compare, but nevertheless, very specific. That it?' The papers were being moved again.

'Nearly. You say that the killer was left-handed. Is there any chance, any chance at all that they could be right-handed?'

'Read my report when you get it. No chance at all. The victim was crouched down, probably on all fours. The killer approached from behind and stabbed from the right side of the victim with their left hand. The trajectory doesn't work right-handed. Read my report, MacLean.' Martha ended the call.

Daisy came and stood next to Callum, her phone still in her hand from her own call. 'Susie Treadwell is downstairs, with her uncle, asking to see you.'

'Let's go and see what she wants.' Callum held open the door and she preceded him into the corridor.

'I dropped in on Rain,' Daisy said.

'How is she?' Callum had not received a summons from her for assistance so had to assume that no news was good news. But it had not stopped him worrying about her.

'Good. She's one tough cookie, Callum. I couldn't quite understand the decrease for the hat I'm knitting, and she had a look at the pattern for me. I offered to make her a cup of tea while she was doing it.' She grinned at Callum. 'I suggest you don't make the same mistake. She said use it–'

'Or lose it,' Callum finished for her. 'Mistake already made. Not to be repeated.'

Daisy laughed. 'She was sitting on the sofa with a load of yarn all around her when I got there. Amber was sitting next to her and was trying to steal the balls. It was quite funny really.' She tipped her head to one side as they neared reception. 'It's good that she likes your cat, isn't it?'

'Is it?' She was fishing for information. She would find out soon enough if Rain agreed to move into Hope Cottage with him.

'Oh well,' she said when he didn't reply.

* * *

Callum took a moment to examine the two figures sitting in the reception area before he and Daisy went out to join them. Susie was enveloped in a man-sized chunky woollen sweater with a ban-the-bomb motif in yellow on the front, a bobble hat and matching scarf in orange and yellow stripes and knitted gloves. She would be easy to spot in a crowd. Uncle Vinny was wearing the raincoat with the greasy lining, but the sleeves were no longer folded back on themselves.

They both rose to their feet when the detectives joined them, but only Susie greeted them with a smile.

Ushered into a vacant room, Susie looked around with curiosity before sliding onto a chair on one side of the table. Uncle Vinny showed no interest in his surroundings as he sat beside her and Callum sensed that he seemed familiar with the insides of an interview room. The space smelled strongly of disinfectant.

'Uncle Vinny said we should come and tell you what we saw,' Susie said, glancing at her uncle.

Callum glanced at him too, but Vinny didn't make eye contact, he just sat back in his chair and folded his arms.

'What did you see, and when did you see it?' Callum asked her.

Susie leaned forward and rested her arms on the table. The left cuff of the jumper had started to unravel.

'It was on the Friday that the man was killed. Me and… I mean Uncle Vinny and I drove up to the telephone box because I needed another book and he offered to come and help me choose.'

'What did you choose?' Callum said, hoping to engage Vinny in the exchange.

'I got two, actually. *The Giver of Stars* by Jojo Moyes – I'm not sure I'm going to like that one – and *Far from the Madding Crowd* by Thomas Hardy.'

'You'll love the descriptions of the settings and characters in that one. I think you'll particularly like Bathsheba Everdene,' Vinny said. His voice was warm and engaging, a surprisingly full-bodied baritone for a man with so light a frame.

'Hmm.' Susie pushed her fringe back under her hat with a gloved finger. 'We were just getting back into the car, and it was quarter to eight, because Uncle Vinny was treating us all to a Chinese and we had to collect it at eight o'clock in Fordingbridge.'

Callum looked at Vinny and he gave a shallow nod of confirmation.

'What did you see?'

'I'm getting to that.' Susie lifted her chin and wriggled on her chair.

Callum thought she was enjoying being the centre of attention.

'A man came along the verge and went into the village hall.'

'Do you know who he was?' Callum asked.

'Of course,' Susie said with a little shake of her head that caused her fringe to escape from her hat. 'When he opened the hall door to go in, the light spilled out and he was easy to see. It was Mr Garland, from the B&B.'

'And you're sure?'

'Of course. And I heard it was him, too, because he called hello to the old lady walking her dogs who was just crossing over the road to go to the B&B.'

Callum glanced at Daisy, and she gave a shallow shrug. Cookie had not mentioned anything about an old woman walking her dogs in his house-to-house report.

'Did you recognise the lady? Have you seen her before?' Callum asked.

'No. I don't think so.'

Vinny stirred. 'Have you finished with us?' His tone was dismissive. Without waiting for Callum's reply, he got to his feet and tapped Susie on the shoulder. 'Home, girl.'

Callum opened the door for them. Susie walked out first, one hand pushing back her hat that was threatening to slide down over her eyes. As Vinny walked past, Callum said, 'Thank you for bringing Susie in and for the information.'

Without breaking stride, Vinny said, 'I know what's right, but no one said I had to like doing it.'

* * *

Bird was on his feet as soon as Callum and Daisy walked through the door into the office.

'His bleedin' alibi is good, guv. Keiron was playing in a skittles match in Ringwood and half the punters saw him. He was there from about quarter past seven, and he couldn't have left if he wanted to because a couple of the others boxed him in. He was nearly the last to leave at closing time.'

'And,' Legs said, coming to join them, 'he is definitely right-handed.'

'Release him,' Callum said. 'Bird, bring in George Garland.'

Callum went into the fishbowl. Behind him, he heard Daisy sharing the information about George and the dog walker. He was annoyed that George had lied to them. Callum thought back. Had anyone asked George if he had left the hall? They had asked him where he was before the meeting, not once it had started.

Chapter Thirty-Seven

George had appeared bemused when asked to accompany the officers to the station but had willingly complied. In the interview room, he sat squarely on his chair, arms resting on the table in front of him, his hands linked loosely together. His glance flicked from Callum to Daisy and back again.

'Should I have a solicitor?' he asked.

'We can wait while you arrange one, if you think you need one,' Daisy said.

'I don't think I need one.' George looked Callum in the eye. 'I've done nothing wrong, Inspector.' The ring he wore on his left hand was polished black titanium with a brushed spinner band set in a flush channel. With the thumb and middle finger of his right hand he rotated the spinner.

'How well did you know Brendan Stafford?' Callum asked.

George stopped touching his ring. 'I didn't. I had no idea the man existed until Abigail told me who he was yesterday.'

'I find that very difficult to believe,' Daisy said. 'You adopted two of his daughters.'

'I adopted two of Abigail's daughters. I never knew who their father was. It didn't matter to me.' A faint madder tinge crept up his neck.

'And if you had known?' Callum asked.

George met his gaze unflinchingly. 'But I didn't know. You are inviting me to speculate, and speculation is not fact. It is just a waste of time.' He sat back in his chair and folded his arms.

Callum nodded at Daisy to continue with her questions.

'Why did you lie about leaving the village hall after the meeting had started?' Daisy asked.

George smiled, unfolded his arms and rested his forearms back on the table. 'Look, Sergeant. We seem to have rather gotten off on the wrong foot here. I never lied about leaving the meeting. You only asked me to account for myself before the meeting started.'

'So why did you leave once it had started?' Daisy persisted. 'Had you arranged to meet Brendan Stafford? Why did you go back home?'

His response was instant. 'Because Abi had left the list of people donating cups for the showjumping classes on the kitchen table by mistake.' There was no tension in his voice, but he resumed spinning his ring. 'Just before we left home, Abi had added Penny Hopwood to her list for the under-twelves cup and then forgot to put it back in the file.' George was calm and earnest, and Callum had a strong misgiving about him killing Brendan despite the fact that he was in the right place at the right time and on his own.

He was sure that George would have overheard Percy telling them about Donny chasing Brendan down the track when he had been arrested earlier in the Garlands' yard. And here George was, admitting that he had been in the same place at about the same time. Not the words of a guilty man. A guilty man would have been putting as much distance between the victim and himself as possible.

'Did you see anybody when you went back to your house?' Daisy asked.

'As I got to the yard, the Palmer brothers were just pulling out onto the driveway. I expect they were going out for supper. Abi doesn't serve evening meals.' He frowned. 'Then I went into the kitchen for the list. The dogs barked at me. I picked up the piece of paper and went back outside. There was a fox barking somewhere close to us, so I quickly checked that Abi had shut the chickens in, and she had, so I went back up the lane to the road.'

'Did you see Keiron on either journey?'

George shook his head. 'No. He'd already left by then.'

'Left the hall?' Daisy asked.

'Yes. He came and signed in before the meeting began, but he's had a falling out with Penny and when she came into the hall just after him, he upped and left almost right away. Abi will confirm that.'

'And you didn't see anybody else on your way to or from your farm?' Daisy asked.

'I didn't have a torch with me, because it was just across the road from home, but I don't remember seeing anybody else, except Olga Brewster, of course. She was close to our drive when I opened the hall door. She always buys eggs from Abi, so I expect that's where she was heading. I probably said good evening to her as I went back into the hall. I was only gone for less than five minutes.'

* * *

'I don't reckon it's George, sir,' Daisy said as they gathered round the board.

'He admitted to being there,' Cookie said.

'No chance that the Palmers, or rather Donny, did it?' Legs said.

'No, doesn't feel right,' Bird said. 'The way Percy feels about Donny at the minute, if he had a shred of evidence against his brother, he would be handing it over to us. I think he's had enough of being bullied by his brother and he's looking to us to rescue him. If he had any evidence, we'd already know about it.'

'Bird's right,' Callum said. 'Percy is angling for a reduced sentence by telling us everything he can think of.'

Bird folded his arms. 'He has given us so much info on how they selected their targets, and broke into the properties, that I could write a bleedin' manual for burglars.'

'Who are our suspects?' Callum said, ignoring Bird's comment.

'We've run out of them,' Daisy said.

'Then we've missed something,' Callum said. He thought for a moment. 'What do we know about Olga Brewster?'

'That she's elderly, a widow; her daughter, Nadia, died; she moved down here when her husband died; she has two dogs and buys eggs from Abigail,' Legs said.

'And you said you thought she might be losing it a bit,' Daisy said.

'No, I just said that standing out in the freezing cold talking to a headstone seems a bit odd. That doesn't make her a murderer. What's her motive?' Legs said. 'He had even paid in advance to stay with her for a bit longer.'

Daisy shrugged.

'Ping.' Cookie flicked his finger against his curls and scooted back to his desk. They all watched him.

'Cookie?' Callum heard the irritation in his own voice, but he was not in the mood for Cookie's antics.

Cookie looked round at them, a broad grin on his face. He hurried back to the board with such speed that the ends of his Indiana Jones tie flapped over his shoulder like trailing kite tails.

'Nadia. Nadia Crapper. Ping. I nearly missed it. I thought it rang a bell.'

'Cookie,' Callum said, his voice louder than he intended. 'What are you talking about?'

'About Brewster being Olga's maiden name. I remember checking and, when she came down here to start her B&B, she reverted to her maiden name,' Cookie said.

'I don't think I'd fancy being called Daisy Crapper. I probably wouldn't change it in the first place,' Daisy said.

Cookie laughed. 'It was one of the names that popped up when you told me to look at Brendan's past,' he said. 'I found it on his social media pages.' He held out a sheet of paper to Bird. 'That's her. That's Nadia Crapper.'

Callum glanced across at the picture. A pretty girl laughed back at him, her eyes full of youthful confidence and naivety. He felt a muscle tug in his cheek and unclenched his jaw.

'She looks like she's just enjoying life,' Daisy said, head tilted as she scrutinised the picture.

'And now she's dead,' Legs said. 'Olga never told me how she died.'

'I know how.' Cookie stood in front of the picture and for a rare moment, even his curls were still. 'She committed suicide.'

'Poor Nadia. Poor Olga,' Legs said quietly.

The muscle in Callum's cheek pulsed, and he said quietly, 'Daisy and I will go and see Olga Brewster.'

* * *

Daisy drove through Criddlestyle along the winding road to Godshill. The rising wind was shaking moisture from the leafless branches that overhung the road, and twice her windscreen wipers swept across the damp glass. For once she had little to say. Callum looked across at her tight features as she rumbled over the cattle grid into the New Forest. She slowed as they approached the pub and indicated to turn onto the road through Godshill village.

'No Susie today,' she said as they passed the empty bus shelter.

Daisy turned off the road onto a gravel track, low-hedged and overhung by oak trees. The cottage on the other side of the boundary was brick-built with what had once been a green oak frame that dissected the walls into smaller sections. As the timber had dried over the intervening years it had hardened and twisted, giving the cottage a patchwork look to it. The building was thatched, and the newly replaced ridge made the old thatch look a tired grey. Smoke curled from a tall chimney in the centre of the roof.

Olga stood in the garden looking down at something in the frost-starched border, her arms wrapped around her body. When Callum and Daisy joined her, they saw that it was a shrine; a small headstone marked Nadia with a pink plastic rose perched on top of it. A copper urn stood in front of the stone with a black silhouette of a girl's head facing them. Olga seemed unaware of the cutting breeze that felt sharp enough to slice the skin and draw blood.

She looked up at them as they approached. 'It was Nadia's birthday last Friday.'

They followed her into her cottage. Daisy stood in front of the window as the others moved deeper into the room.

Olga Brewster's sitting room was exactly as Legs had described it, pink roses and photos. Olga lowered herself into an armchair and wrapped a blanket around her shoulders. She shivered now and again, Callum assumed from getting cold in the garden, but she seemed otherwise calm. There was a faraway look in her eyes when she raised her head as if she was looking past Callum to something beyond him. He wondered if she was fully aware of what was happening.

Callum sat on the sofa facing Olga, his head now more on a level with hers. 'Mrs Brewster,' he said. 'We need to ask you some questions.'

She looked at him, then lifted a framed photo from a side table. Her thumb gently caressed the scrolled silver edging before she turned it around for him to view.

'That is my Nadia.' She held it steady, giving Callum an opportunity to admire the young woman's face. It had a more serious expression than the image that Cookie had found on social media. Olga turned it back to face her and then hugged the photo to her chest. 'It was her birthday last Friday.'

Callum registered the repeated information, sat back in his seat and motioned Daisy to stay where she was, standing behind Olga's chair, next to the window.

'Her best friend from college, Sally, always rings me on Nadia's birthday. She misses Nadia almost as much as I do.' Olga began to rock backwards and forwards. 'After breakfast on Friday, when Brendan had already gone out, Sally rang me, and we had a good old natter. You won't understand but, talking to Sally is like going back, as if Nadia might walk through the door any second.'

Callum's phone vibrated in his pocket. Daisy glanced at her screen, looked across at him, and gave a slight shake of her head advising him that it was nothing that required immediate action.

'Sally still lives in the next street from our old house. I couldn't stay there after Nadia killed herself. I kept seeing her in the shadows, I had dreams where I was trying to revive her, I heard her voice calling me on the wind and worse, every room I went into, I could smell her perfume. It was as if she was haunting me, trying to cling to me, even though she was gone.'

Callum looked down at his folded hands. He understood perfectly.

Olga stopped rocking and sat up straight. 'That's why we had to move away from Birmingham. Stan never really got over her death. She was very precious to us, you see. He drove into a tree late one night and died.' She released the photo from her tight clutch and looked down at it. 'My angel.' A tear landed on the glass surface.

Callum looked up at Daisy, who was holding her bottom lip between her teeth.

'I had never known the name of the man who had hurt her so deeply that she couldn't face life when he abandoned her. But Sally has always known and last Friday, for the first time, she told me his name. It was Brendan Stafford.' Olga took a shaky breath. 'After our phone call was over, I spent a long time in the garden talking to Nadia and we decided that it would be best if I asked him to leave us when he came back that evening. We talked for a long time, and I must have got a little cold outside because I fell asleep in my chair. The dogs woke me because they wanted to be fed. It was dark outside.'

'Where are your dogs?' Daisy asked, looking around the room. Callum frowned at her for interrupting.

'My friend has them. She is going to look after them.' Olga glanced around at Daisy.

'You took your dogs for a walk when you woke up,' Callum prompted in a gentle voice and Olga turned back to face him.

'I took them for a walk. I decided to return the tool that Keiron left here when he was repairing my ridge, and I needed eggs. Kill two birds.' She took a trembling breath. 'I was nearly at Abigail's when I walked past the village hall. George was just going in the door, and he saw me and said hello. I crossed over the road and went down his lane and the lights came on when I got to their yard.' She slowed the narrative as if she was trying to be sure that she recounted every detail. 'I was going to get rid of the tool first and then get my eggs. I walked down the track and when I got near the barns the outside lights came on. That's when I saw him, on all fours on the track with his jacket pulled up over his shoulders. He had his back towards me.'

She looked at Callum. 'I'm sorry for what I did next. All I could see was Nadia on the floor as I tried to resuscitate her.' The skin of Olga's face stretched tight. 'I hit him as hard as I could.' She thumped her fist down on her own knee. 'That's for Nadia, I told him.' Her tears were silent, seeping into the fissures of her face like a quietly incoming tide. 'What sort of man is he? He hadn't even recognised her when he saw her in all my photos. I didn't know the thatch thing was in my hand.' She looked down at her hand and her breath snagged in her throat. 'Then, when I stepped back, I saw it sticking out of his back. I pulled it out and threw it over at Keiron's barn.' Her breaths were shallow sobs that deepened until her shoulders jerked upwards, her ribs spasmed and her upper body fell forward.

Daisy came towards them and Callum reached out a hand and placed it on Olga's shoulder. She smelt of roses and her bones felt fragile beneath his fingers. He closed his eyes briefly and banished a memory.

'Take a deep breath,' he said. He watched as she struggled to follow his advice. 'Again,' he said when she managed to comply. He looked up at Daisy who had come to stand beside Olga.

'That text was Cookie,' Daisy said, kneeling on the floor next to Olga. 'They've just found the reeding pin at the barn.'

Chapter Thirty-Eight

'Poor Olga,' Daisy said. 'Finding out that he was sleeping in the next room to her at night pushed her over the edge, I reckon.'

'That and feeling disrespectful to Nadia by looking after Brendan. She must have felt so cheated,' Legs said, folding her arms across her yellow top.

'Doesn't give her the right to go popping holes in him though,' Bird added.

Callum moved across the office to join them. 'That was an excellent result today; well done, people. We've arrested two burglars and retrieved, as far as we can assess, all of the stolen property.'

'Including the ever so important golf prize,' Daisy said with a grin.

'And we have found the killer of Brendan Stafford,' Callum said. He registered the sudden stillness and moment of silence.

Bird cleared his throat but didn't speak.

'I thought you would be interested to know that there is a possibility that Olga will be charged with manslaughter, not murder. The feeling is that she was mentally unwell at the time she committed the offence,' Callum said.

'I'd be feeling mentally unwell too if I found I was sharing a house with the bloke I bleedin' held responsible for my daughter's death,' Bird said.

'You mean her suffering mentally affected her ability to make a rational judgement,' Daisy said. 'That I can understand.'

'Yeah, but you still can't go round killing people,' Cookie said. He wielded an imaginary épée, lunged forward and shouted, 'En garde.' Then he tripped and cannoned into the back of a chair, tipping Bird forward against his desk.

'Seems like a bleedin' good idea right now,' Bird said, righting himself, and Legs and Daisy laughed.

* * *

Callum opened his front door. Rain was talking to someone in the living room. He clicked closed the door.

'Hello,' she called.

'Hello yourself,' he answered from the hall. 'I thought you had company,' he said with surprise as he went into the sitting room and saw that she was sitting alone on the sofa. She turned down the volume on the quiz programme she was watching. Her colour was much better than when she had woken that morning, but her bruises had taken on deeper hues.

'I have got company.' Rain pointed at Amber who was sitting on the rag rug at her feet. 'We were having a theoretical discussion on the merits of working with dry wool, versus wet and chewed wool. Our preferences differ.'

Amber made small noises in her throat and went to Callum to rub her head against his legs.

'Are you being a nuisance, you bonnie wee beastie?'

'I think we've come to an understanding after our lengthy discussion,' Rain said with mock seriousness, then laughed as Amber stretched out her leg, hooked a ball of yarn towards her and made off with it.

'Further negotiations needed, I think,' Callum said. 'Cup of tea?' He took the ball of wool from Amber and tossed it back to Rain who deftly caught it.

'Please.'

'How have you been today?' he asked as he filled the kettle.

'Good. Better than I'd hoped, to be honest. I shall think all our patients are malingerers from now on.' She began putting the yarn into her butterfly-decorated bag. 'It was nice to see Daisy. Did you ask her to come?'

'She volunteered. She had some unfathomable query about a knitting pattern for a hat that she's making herself for this cold snap.' He dropped teabags in the mugs and spluttered boiling water on top of them. 'The weather is going to get warmer next week so I don't think she's going to need it.' He passed her a mug of tea.

'She'll be fine. She's enjoying the project and extending her skill base at the same time.' Rain tied the handles in a loose knot at the top of the full bag of yarn and placed it on the coffee table before leaning back in her chair. She looked up at him and smiled. 'Why are you staring me?'

'No reason.' The red leather emitted a squeak as he sat next to her on the sofa.

'It's nice that you're home. I missed you.' She picked up her mug and looked at him over the rim as she took a sip of liquid.

'Me too.' He placed a hand on her knee.

They both spoke at the same time, then both fell silent.

'You first,' Rain said.

Callum shook his head. 'Ladies first.' He cupped his hands around his mug and sipped his tea; eyes fixed on her face.

'Okay, but it's nothing important. I was wondering if you were intending us to eat the steak in the fridge for supper, or if you were saving it for some sort of special meal.'

‘A bit of both,’ he said. His blood was flushing trepidation through his veins, building suspense that was worse than any disappointment he might have to cope with. His rehearsed words chased through his brain. He took a breath and forgot every one of them. ‘Rain, will you move in with me?’

‘At last,’ she said. ‘I thought you were never going to ask me. I must get run over more often.’

‘Please don’t,’ he whispered. ‘Really, please don’t.’

THE END

Character List

The Team

DI Callum MacLean –Relocated from Glasgow to the New Forest in 2020

DS Daisy Donaldson (Deedee) – Single, loves all animals

DC Almadia Levens (Legs) – Nigerian officer from Liverpool. Married to Gloria

DC Thomas Cooke (Cookie) – Youngest member of the team

DC Tony Hampton (Bird) – Ex-military, rescues injured birds

DCI Bertram Bellman – Callum's immediate superior officer

Dr Martha Jones – Doctor

Others

Abigail Garland – Gymkhana show secretary and owner of Crossways Farm B&B

Brendan Stafford – Retired lecturer

Bethany – Friend of Rain

Charlotte Garland (Charlie) – Daughter of Abigail and George

Darcie Garland – Daughter of Abigail and George

Donald Snow (Dancer) – Member of the Reindeer Gang

Daphne Smart – Retired headmistress

Emilia Garland (Ems) – Daughter of Abigail and George

Eddie Gilligan – Local forestry worker

Elsie Bridewell – Burglary victim

Felicity Garland (Flissa) – Daughter of Abigail and George

Finn Lewis – Landlord of the Drunken Donkey

George Garland – Local businessman and owner of Crossways Farm B&B. Married to Abigail Garland

Glynn Roberts – Burglary victim

Harry Kingman – Butcher

Irene Kingman – Harry's wife

Janey – Mother of Susie Treadwell

Jimmy Eastwood – Local agister

Keiron Tapper – Thatcher

Lucas Norton – Estate agent

Miles Samways – Friend of Eddie

Mickey Palmer – Birdwatcher

Olga Brewster – Owner of Willow Cottage B&B

Penny Hopwood – Hurdle maker

Percy Snow (Prancer) – Member of the Reindeer Gang

Rainbow Waters (Rain) – Callum's partner

Susie Treadwell – Avid reader

Stella Lewis – Landlady of the Drunken Donkey

Sebastian Wells – Friend of Eddie

Tom Palmer – Birdwatcher

Victoria Stafford – Ex-wife of Brendan Stafford

Vinny – Susie's uncle

Acknowledgements

I want to thank two groups of writers who have provided critique and encouragement in equal measures. The first are Lisa, Sandra, Valerie, Penny and Jan, and the second are Emma, Sam, Zab, Veronica, Tracy and Caroline. They are all writers, and I am privileged to have their support.

Thanks also to my beta readers, especially Helen who provides excellent coffee. To Hugh Bond and Dr Cathy Wield MBBS MRCEM for answering my questions on all things medical and to Forestry England for providing information on the New Forest.

This would have been a very different book without the input of all these people, and I cannot overestimate the importance of them all to the finished novel.

My gratitude goes to the team at The Book Folks who have been all-round amazing and a pleasure to work with, and especially Polly for her extreme patience.

My special thanks go to my husband and son for their endless enthusiasm, unstinting support and their belief in me.

I hope you enjoy this crime novel and that reading about the New Forest will encourage you to come and visit us.

The Book Folks & Joffe Books Story

The Book Folks began in 2013, founded by Erik Empson with a simple but powerful goal — to publish highly readable, compelling fiction that readers would love. With a focus on crime fiction, thrillers and gripping mysteries, The Book Folks quickly built a loyal audience and became known for championing talented authors from the UK, Ireland, the US and beyond.

From gritty police procedurals and psychological thrillers to fast-paced action and suspense, The Book Folks earned a reputation for curating addictive stories at affordable prices — often introducing readers to hidden gems and breakout talent.

In 2025, The Book Folks proudly became part of Joffe Books, the UK's largest independent publisher. Joffe Books started in 2014 when Jasper Joffe published his mum's long-rejected romance novel — which unexpectedly became a bestseller. That spirit of risk-taking and reader-first publishing has defined Joffe Books ever since.

Together, Joffe Books and The Book Folks are united by a passion for page-turning fiction and a deep respect for the authors who create it. We're proud to publish some of the best-loved names in fiction — including Joy Ellis, Faith Martin, Caro Ramsay, Simon Brett, Helen Forrester, and Robert Goddard — as well as fresh voices bringing new energy to the genre.

We never forget that everything begins with the author's story — and that continues with you, the reader.

We love hearing from you, so get in touch any time at feedback@joffebooks.com.

And if you'd like to receive free books and hear about our latest releases, sign up to our newsletter:
www.joffebooks.com/freebooks

Thanks for reading — and for being part of our story.

www.thebookfolks.com

Printed in Dunstable, United Kingdom

67670897R00139